Whispers of Forgiveness
Book One in the Whispers of New England Series
Sue Mills

Choose the Front Row Media

"What if you got another chance with your first love?

Quinn and Sam were everything to each other for years, before their relationship met a bitter end in college. When they see each other again for the first time in ten years, they have a chance to put the past to rest and reclaim their friendship—but as they continue to spend time together, their intense attraction becomes as undeniable as it is inconvenient.

Slow-burn fans will enjoy this steamy second-chance love story." Mary M., Line Editor, Red Adept Editing

DEDICATION

If you've ever hoped for the chance to try again...
Or even the opportunity for a proper good-bye, this is for you

Contents

Chapter 1
The Empty Seat

Quinn

Quinn Michaels's head snapped up as footsteps sounded behind her in the darkened auditorium. She was sitting on the aisle at a conference titled Healthy Living in the Workplace, and the lecture hall was packed for introductions and the keynote address. Her early arrival had been timed to give her a choice of where to sit, and relief surged over her when the lights dimmed and the adjacent seat was still empty. The footsteps drew closer.

The loser who just walked in forty-five minutes late is going to want that empty spot.

She had placed her tote bag on the vacant seat, hoping to keep it for herself. *I hate how I still try to isolate myself in crowds.* When she was younger, she'd been an awkward and introverted teenager with few friends. Athletic, but heavier than she wanted to be, she had envied her thinner teammates. The ten years since her high school graduation had seen her fulfill her dream of becoming a registered nurse and living far from her hometown in rural Vermont. After five years in Virginia and three in Seattle, Quinn had returned to New England, where, to her surprise, she finally felt at home. She'd cultivated the powerful circle of friends that she'd always craved and had recently become the wellness coordinator for her floor at the hospital. Those extra pounds that plagued her in high school had turned into lush curves. She was confident and caring, but the insecure teenager still bubbled to the surface in unfamiliar situations, like this work conference.

Quinn felt the tap on her shoulder. "Dammit." She moved her tote bag and swung her legs into the aisle, turning her head as the latecomer squeezed by. *What kind of person walks into a conference nearly an hour late?*

The man now seated next to her was breathing like he'd run a marathon. Quinn sighed. She was still aggravated, but that didn't overshadow her sympathy for the guy. She suspected the weekday Boston traffic probably did him in.

The Sunday drive to her hotel the day before, by contrast, had been pleasant. It was early November, and the trees in Massachusetts were just beginning to lose their bright-orange and golden-yellow leaves. New England's autumn riot of color warmed her soul; it was what she had missed the most living in Seattle. Football season was in full swing, contributing to the mostly empty streets. The majority of people were at home or in a bar, watching the Patriots.

Turning her head slightly to look at the latecomer, she found him with his elbows on his knees and his head in his hands. He seemed wiry, but Quinn could see the outline of his bicep through his gray shirt. His brown hair was short and his hands caught her attention. Her stomach jumped with the realization that he looked a lot like Sam Carpenter, her high school boyfriend. She couldn't see his face, but the hair, his build, the angle of his neck, and those hands all reminded her of Sam. Her head whipped back around. *No! There's no way Sam would be at a conference like this.*

She tried to look again without being obvious, but his face was still buried in his hands.

Her heart pounded wildly, and the heat of panic flooded her body. *I've got to get out of here!*

Sam

Sam Carpenter had just lived through the worst morning of his life. As he was walking out the door, Norah, his partner of eight years, had said, "Piper and I won't be here when you get back. I've rented a house, and I thought it would be easier for her if we move while you're away."

Sam froze in his tracks. Turning around, his stomach churning, he went back inside. "What? With no discussion?"

She reminded him they had agreed in counseling that separating would be best then added, "But you've done nothing to make that happen. In typical Sam fashion, you think if you ignore something, it will go away."

Her voice was filled with bitterness, and he was glad Piper, their six-year-old daughter, was still asleep so she wasn't subjected to yet another argument.

"I've gone to every counseling session, done everything that's been suggested. What more do you want?"

Her expression softened, but her gray eyes were filled with steely resolve. "I wanted you to leave."

"I'm not leaving this house, Norah. Not after all the work I've put into it. And it's the only home that Pip has known!"

"Since you won't do anything, I have."

Sam recognized the silent accusation in her words, her belief that he *never* did anything.

"Piper will adjust to another home. We'll talk when you get back about visitation and sorting out our finances. You need to be on your way. You're going to be late. As usual." With that, she literally pushed him out the door.

Her words had played in Sam's head over and over—*Piper and I won't be here when you get back*—as he drove away. He stopped at the first rest area he came to, near Lebanon, New Hampshire, just twenty miles from his house, and stood by the side of the car in turmoil.

Should I have stayed? Should I go back? Would it make any difference? Norah has her mind made up. He sighed. *Nothing I say or do is going to change anything.*

And I have an obligation to my job. He rubbed the back of his neck. *Damn it.* Sam thought of his father, who'd instilled a strict work ethic in his son. *I should go.*

Still unsure, Sam checked the time. His boss, John, had told him the opening address wasn't important, which was why he hadn't driven down the night before. But John definitely wanted Sam there for the afternoon sessions, and he'd highly recommended the keynote speaker. He'd be on time for the keynote if he left for the hotel now—unless the traffic was truly as bad as everyone had told him it would be.

He pulled out his cell to call Jesse, his best friend. "Hey, Jesse. You will not believe this. Norah's moving out while I'm away. She laid it on me as I was walking out the door!" His voice broke. "I fucking can't believe it. Are you still going to be at the conference tomorrow? I'd like to talk to you."

Jesse had sent back a text saying he'd be there on Tuesday and suggested they get together for lunch.

Sam slammed his hand on the hood of the car in frustration before climbing back in and continuing on his way, still hearing Norah's voice during the entire drive from central Vermont to Boston. The city skyline was barely visible when the cars in front of him came to an abrupt stop. He'd never been to Boston, and the tangle of cars was far beyond anything he could have imagined. The stress of the traffic finally silenced Norah's voice.

Once he made it through the traffic snarl, the car's navigation directed him to the hotel garage, where he spent precious minutes searching for an open spot. When the car was finally parked, he speed-walked to the conference center.

By the time Sam sat down in the only open seat in the darkened lecture hall, he was out of breath and frazzled. Resting his elbows on his thighs with his face in his hands, he struggled to get himself under control. After a few minutes, he slumped back, staring straight ahead and hearing Norah's words again. *Piper and I won't be here...*

He shoved them from his mind and tried to focus on the stage, but his mind still wandered. *Damn, this place is huge, and there's a shit ton of people here. I'll never find my way around. I should never have agreed to coordinate wellness activities for the office.*

The lights came on, signaling a break. *I hope this chick next to me stands up. I desperately need to pee, and I don't want to waste a second squeezing by her.*

The woman stood, moving into the aisle, and Sam hurried out of the row, throwing a glance toward her, then stopped in his tracks. *No way.*

That could be Quinn.

He took several steps, but the sense of recognition grew stronger. Then he turned, walking back toward the woman, raising his eyes quizzically, his need for a bathroom forgotten.

"Quinn?" he asked.

After a second, she nodded.

He shook his head. "My God, you're the last person I expected to run into."

Quinn shrugged her shoulders, and a faint red hue colored her face. It reminded him of their first meeting back in high school, which had left her tongue-tied.

They stared at each other as they stood silently in the swirl of people going to buy coffee or find a restroom.

Should I hug her? I want to hug her. That's what you do when you run into old friends, right? Something in her demeanor made him hesitate.

She drew a deep breath. "I'm headed to the restroom."

"Yeah, me, too, and I..." Stammering, unsure what to say next, he finally continued, "I need to sign in at the registration table. I was a little late getting here." A self-deprecating grin escaped his lips. "I'd like to catch up."

She shrugged again and started toward the auditorium door.

Sam headed to the restroom, trying to remember the details of Quinn's life now. He'd thought she was living on the West Coast.

The lights flickered as he returned to the auditorium, signaling that the keynote speaker was making his way to the stage.

Sam took his seat and leaned over to whisper in Quinn's ear, "Can we talk when this guy is done?"

Chapter 2
Reminiscing

Sam

SAM HEARD NOTHING THE speaker said as he remembered the day he met Quinn.

It had been the first day of school. He had been climbing the stairs to the first class of his senior year when the girl ahead of him stumbled and ended up falling into his arms. He steadied her, noticing her long, dark hair, her warm brown eyes, and the furious blush that overtook her face.

She'd scrambled away from him without saying a word.

Extremely cute, Sam thought, *but too young for me.*

Entering his health class, he realized there were no other seniors in the room. *Damn, I should have taken this two years ago, like Joe told me to.* Silently, he cursed himself for not listening to his older brother.

Sam was the middle child of three boys from a family known as hard workers—high praise in their small Vermont town.

School was a challenge, but he studied diligently and was hoping to be the first in his family to attend college. His cool-blue eyes, combined with his wavy, light-brown hair, had been attracting female attention since his freshman year. Girls flirted with him all the time, but his parents were strict about him having a job and doing well in school. He had turned eighteen a week before school started, but unlike some classmates who thought reaching that age set them free from parental rule, Sam knew better than to challenge his father. He had no time for a girlfriend.

The class was ready to start when the girl from the stairs walked in. He recognized her immediately. The only open seat was next to him, and she hesitantly made her way to it.

He said, "Are you okay? I'm Sam Carpenter."

Her face reddened, and she seemed unable to utter a word.

Sam was intrigued. The teacher took attendance, and that was how he learned her name: Quinn Michaels.

Sam's personality was outgoing and engaging, the complete opposite of Quinn, who was quiet and introverted. He was friendly to her, talking and joking before and after class, trying to draw her out. Eventually, she became comfortable with him. They exchanged cell numbers and texted late into the night.

As fall turned to winter, Sam's anticipation for the downhill ski season was high. He had been on the ski team since his freshman year and would be one of the captains. It surprised him to see Quinn there on the first day of tryouts. Skiing had not come up in their conversations, and Sam was amazed by how fast and fearless she was on the slopes. It was the opposite of her everyday demeanor. He became her mentor, teaching her the ins and outs of the races. Spending time on the slopes, watching her ski and knowing her eyes were on him, was exhilarating and intensified his feelings for her.

Sam wanted to ask her out, but his parents were adamant that she was too young for him. Even his reasoning that Quinn had turned sixteen after the school year started fell on deaf ears. Sam had to be content with text messages and stolen moments at ski meets or during the school day.

Graduation came, and the summer spooled away far too fast for Sam. The only time he saw Quinn was when he went through her checkout line at the grocery store. He offered to do the grocery shopping for his mother more that summer than he ever had before.

Sam knew everything would be different when he left for college. He wouldn't have his parents peering over his shoulder, and he'd be surrounded by women experiencing that same freedom for the first time. Quinn wasn't as shy as she was when they met, and he knew it was only a matter of time until she started dating. He wanted to be her first date, her first kiss. He hated the thought of leaving without experiencing that.

With three weeks left until his departure for college, Sam defied his parents and invited Quinn out on a date. They were surrounded by other diners at the restaurant but only had eyes for each other. After dinner, they went to a movie where they held hands in the darkened theater, thrilled to be together.

After the movie, Sam parked at Quinn's house and opened the car door for her. He raised his hand to cup her cheek while his other arm wrapped around her waist, drawing her close. He lowered his mouth to hers, and their lips melted together.

He felt Quinn sigh, and when he loosened his hold on her, she whispered, "Can we do this again?"

Sam laughed and kissed her again. "You mean this?"

"I mean all of it. I can't believe you're leaving in three weeks."

"Twenty-one days, and I want to see you on every one of them. Will your parents let you?"

"Yes. They want to get to know you after hearing me talk about you non-stop for a year. We can hang out here, go swimming, and have a bonfire. We don't have to spend money. I just want to be with you."

On the fourth night that Sam returned home after midnight, Trent Carpenter had been waiting up. As Sam tiptoed toward the stairs, his father's voice rang out, saying, "Where have you been?"

"Out."

Sam heard a click, and the living room was bathed in light. Trent was nursing a glass of whiskey, and Sam knew it wasn't his first.

Trent pointed at the couch. "Sit. We need to have a chat." His voice was subdued and menacing, which unnerved Sam more than shouting.

Sam took one more step toward his bedroom before taking a deep breath and walking to the couch.

"Again, where have you been?"

"On a date."

"With whom?"

"Dad." Sam sighed. "I'm almost nineteen. I don't need to tell you who I'm dating."

"As long as you're living in this house, you'll answer my questions. Is it that girl you wanted to ask out last fall?"

"Quinn. Her name is Quinn."

"What the hell are you doing? She's sixteen. You realize if you fuck around with her, you could end up in jail."

"You've made that abundantly clear since the first day I mentioned her name."

Trent slammed his empty glass on the table. "Your whole future is in front of you. If you knock her up, you will marry her. Do you understand that?"

"Yes, sir."

His father continued, "That will be the end of all your plans to be a hotshot architect."

"It's not like that. We don't have any plans to have sex."

Trent cupped his hand over his ear. "How old did you say you are? That's right. Nineteen. You think I don't know what boys your age want? You end this now before it goes any further."

"No."

"What?" Trent barked.

"I'm going to continue seeing Quinn until I leave. I've heard your warnings, but you don't need to worry about me."

Trent shook his head. "You're going to disobey me over a piece of ass. Your mother won't let me throw you out, but do not expect any financial support from us while you are seeing her." With that, Trent stood, snapped off the light, and stumbled toward the kitchen.

What his father didn't know was that Sam had already had sex once, more as a rite of passage than an expression of love, and while the release was amazing, it had left him feeling unsatisfied. That wasn't what he wanted with Quinn.

College was three hours away, and Sam made the trip back to their hometown every other weekend. Quinn's parents let him stay in their guest room, and he ended up spending more time at Quinn's house than at his own.

The love between Quinn and Sam grew stronger every time they were together, but with his father's warning echoing in his mind, they did not make love until Quinn turned eighteen, soon after her senior year started.

They had two wonderful years—until Quinn left for college and it all came crashing down.

Quinn

Quinn listened to a few minutes of the speaker before her mind wandered to how she and Sam met and their time dating. She had been a newcomer as a sophomore. Her freshman year had been spent at a bigger school that she quickly realized was not the right fit. She made the decision to transfer despite knowing she'd be walking into a situation where the social groups were already established and the likelihood of making friends was low.

Her anxiety had been sky-high on the first day of school, and falling into Sam Carpenter's arms had done nothing to lessen it. Little did she know that the most embarrassing moment of her life would turn out to be one of the best, as Sam became the only friend she needed.

By the time they finally went on a date, nearly a year after they met, Quinn was already halfway to loving him. They traveled the rest of the road to love together, totally devoted to each other. Sam always treated her with gentleness and respect. Until that last time they were together.

Quinn didn't deny her part in their breakup, but the venom and anger that Sam unleashed that night had shattered her. The only way she'd finally been able to move on was by concentrating on his shortcomings, so she'd grown to regret the time they'd spent together, convincing herself that she was better off without him.

However, Quinn's heart had betrayed her in the convention center when at the mere sight of Sam, it leapt the same way it had when she was fifteen.

Quinn thought about what she knew of Sam's current life. The rumor mill in their small town was very active and had long tentacles that seemed to reach her no matter where she was. The extent of her knowledge was that he'd been with the same woman for several years and had a young daughter.

The speaker finished, and the lights came up. Quinn was startled at how quickly the hour had gone by. Her heart was pounding. She had not been face-to-face with Sam since the end of their relationship. How was she supposed to react? It had been ten years since Sam broke things off with Quinn. *What the hell do we have to talk about?*

They stood and were immediately swept into the crush of people leaving the hall. Quinn could see Sam's mouth moving but had no idea what he was saying as the noisy crowd swirled around them. She raised her hands to her ears and shook her head.

He grabbed the notebook he'd been given at registration and scribbled, *Lunch?*

Quinn shook her head and mouthed, *No, I'm meeting someone.*

He scribbled again. *Dinner then? To catch up?*

The noise was subsiding, so she murmured, "No, I can't."

I could. I don't have plans until tomorrow. But God, how awkward would it be?

The thinning crowd still moved around them as they stood gazing at each other, Quinn locked in indecision.

Sam stared at her with puppy dog eyes and asked, "Please?"

Quinn recognized the begging tone in his voice. *What harm will one dinner do?* She sighed deeply then nodded.

He smiled. "Meet at six in the lobby?"

She hesitated then nodded again.

"I'll give you my cell number." He reached for her cell and held his out for her to take.

Reluctantly, she entered her number into his phone and handed it back to him.

His eyes locked on hers for a few seconds. "You look good, Quinn. It'll be nice to talk to you." Shoving the phone in his pocket, he ambled toward the entrance.

Chapter 3
Spinning in a Million Directions

Sam

Quinn Michaels. I most certainly did not expect to run into her.

Sam had surprised himself by asking her to dinner. And more surprising, she agreed to meet him. His mind spun, still in a Quinn-induced daze, while he walked to the hotel registration desk.

As he stood in line, however, the soundtrack of Norah's words from the morning started up again.

Sam had moved out for a couple of months during the summer, but they had discussed every aspect beforehand. This time, Norah had gone at him with malice. As she'd pushed him out the door, she said they'd have to work out when he could see Piper and how to disentangle their finances. His hands were tied because of his commitment in Boston, preventing him from staying to argue. He had pulled the door shut behind him with a bang that echoed in his head for the first few miles of his drive.

I can't believe she sprung that on me as I was leaving. I feel like that fucking door just slammed shut on our relationship.

He finally reached the front of the line to check into the hotel and got the key to his room on the seventh floor. Next, he headed to the garage, where he wandered through the parked cars clicking his fob, hoping to see lights flickering. He'd been so late that he'd forgotten where he parked.

The hunt for the car was a welcome break. The quiet of the garage gave him an opportunity to process the morning. *Would I have asked Quinn to dinner if Norah had not told me about her plan to move out while I'm away? Yes. There's so much I should say to her. Maybe not dinner but I would have found some way to talk to her.*

Norah was a completely self-assured person. That quality had drawn him to her in the first place. She didn't suffer from internal doubts—except where Quinn Michaels was concerned. They started dating two years after his breakup with Quinn, but Norah had always felt threatened by her.

Finally, the car lights flickered. He grabbed his bag out of the car, then he made his way back to the hotel and up to his room.

Once there, he yanked his running gear out of his duffle and tossed it on the bed. The workshops would end at four, and he wanted to go for a quick run before his dinner date.

No! Not a date. It's two old friends sharing a meal.

In the lobby he found the concierge and asked, "Can you recommend a restaurant within walking distance where I can have a leisurely dinner?"

She smiled, and Sam noticed her dazzling green eyes. *I don't think I've ever seen eyes that color.*

She named a seafood restaurant a short distance away and asked, "Do you want me to make a reservation for you?"

Sam answered in the affirmative, and as the concierge was going online to make the reservation, she asked if he had any special requests.

"Can you ask for a secluded table?" He wasn't hiding, but a quiet spot would be nice. He and Quinn had a lot to catch up on.

Those green eyes locked on his. "You're all set for six thirty. Anything else I can help you with?"

"Yes, can you tell me how to get to Boston Common? I want to go for a run."

She pulled out a map and marked a route that would cover five miles through Boston Common and the Public Garden. She smiled as she handed him the map, and her fingers lingered on his as he took it.

Sam walked away, thinking, *Damn, was she coming onto me? It's been so long—I don't even know if a woman is flirting with me.*

Sam slid into his seat for the afternoon session a few minutes early, savoring the first calm moment he'd felt since he walked out of his house that morning.

His mind went back to Norah's declaration.

I know she doesn't think I pull my share of the weight in the house. She ignores the fact that because she leaves for work so early, I'm the one taking care of getting Piper ready for school—French braiding her hair, making sure her socks match, putting together her lunch, all of it. And I pick her up at the end of the day, take care of any paperwork from the school, cook dinner... I should make a list.

He pulled a spiral bound notebook out of his backpack and opened it to the first blank page. He stared at the page for a few minutes and then sighed. *What am I doing? It's not a competition. That's not how a relationship between two people is supposed to be.*

When Piper was a baby, Sam and Norah had feigned mock fights over who could spend more time with her. They were totally over-the-top in their love for the tiny person they'd made together.

Piper had been a toddler when Norah received a promotion requiring a move to a more distant office as well as more responsibility. Sam's job as a project manager for an economic development council in the town where they lived allowed him greater flexibility than Norah's, and he happily took on the weekday tasks required to get a small human out the door in the morning.

As Norah became more driven and worked more hours, the importance of Sam's contributions to making their lives run smoothly seemed to shrink in Norah's mind. At least, that's how Sam saw it.

The topic of the afternoon session was mentorship, and Sam thought about his friend Jesse and how he had mentored Sam in his first job. Instead of making a list to throw in Norah's face, he used the page to consider who would make good mentors in his office. He jotted down their names and then matched them with new hires who could use some direction.

After that, he turned to the next page in the notebook and started sketching the storage shed he wanted to build at home, as well as the landscaping. He wanted the shed to mirror the style of the house. His pencil flew across the paper, but he was still aware of the speaker and made sure to flip back to his list of mentors whenever he heard an idea that might work in his office.

When did it all start to go south with Norah? Was it that trip to California?

Norah traveled frequently for work, but her trips were usually only for one or two nights. Three years ago, she'd gone to California for a week. When she returned from the trip, Piper had launched herself into Norah's arms as soon as she walked in the door. Still holding Pip, Norah's first words to Sam were, "Did you do anything while I was gone?"

Sam wanted to respond, "Yes, I kept our child alive," but he bit his tongue.

Piper had come down with a twenty-four-hour stomach bug after Norah left on Sunday night. Sam had spent the night cleaning up barf, and Piper stayed on the couch all day Monday. On Tuesday morning, she was better, so he dropped her off at daycare before heading to his office. Mid-afternoon, he received a call that Piper had a fever and he needed to pick her up. The night passed fitfully, and Sam took her to the pediatrician on Wednesday morning. She had an ear infection, so the rest of the week passed with the two of them cuddled on the couch watching countless episodes of her favorite shows. She was on antibiotics, and he alternated giving her acetaminophen and ibuprofen to keep the fever at bay. In between giving her medicine and keeping her comfortable, he managed to finish an important project for work.

So yes, when Norah came home, she saw dirty dishes on the counter because the dishwasher was full of clean ones Sam hadn't had a chance to put away, and there were clean clothes in laundry baskets, waiting to be folded. There were pillows and blankets on the couch, and Piper's stuffed animals were scattered about the living room. He fully acknowledged that the house was something of a disaster area, but Piper was alive and well. Still, Norah was standoffish for the next few weeks.

Sam paused in his sketching as he realized they'd never really come back from that trip. He'd spent the time since that day wondering if there was more to Norah's animosity toward him than just a messy house. The only time since then that things had been good between him and Norah was the past summer when they weren't living together.

The session finished, leaving Sam with a page of ideas for mentorship at his office, a preliminary sketch of the storage building, and unresolved questions about what his future would be like.

Sam rushed back to his room and threw on his running clothes. He grabbed the map the concierge had given him and made his way outside. It was a beautiful day for early November, close to fifty degrees and sunny. He rarely ran during the week once summer was over because by the time he left the office and picked up Piper, it was too dark to run on their narrow country road.

Running in the city, however, was a whole new experience. Leaving the hotel, he threaded his way along a sidewalk jammed with people. Boston Common proved to be less crowded with wider paths. His thoughts drifted, but because it was unfamiliar territory, he tried to keep his mind focused on his route.

The duckling statues from the book *Make Way for Ducklings* loomed in front of him with kids climbing all over them and smiling parents taking their pictures. The kids were jockeying for position on the mama duck and grinning broadly for the cameras. He paused to watch for a few minutes. *I'd love to do that with Pip.*

Less than twenty-four hours had gone by, and he already missed Piper. He'd only spent a couple of nights away from her, which made Norah's plan to move harder to take.

What is it going to be like not putting her to bed every night or having her jump on me in the morning? His pace quickened as the morning's Norah soundtrack started playing again.

Back at the hotel, Sam caught his breath and did some stretches. The run had taken care of some of the tension he'd been feeling, and Sam knew he wanted to do it again, maybe in the morning. When he entered the hotel, he noticed the concierge. She stood in front of the desk, and her long legs and blond hair captured his attention.

She caught his eye and smiled. *She's flirting. Do I have a sign on my back? "Got dumped this morning." Women don't generally flirt with me.*

Sam entered his room, peeled off his sweaty shirt, and thought about calling Piper. *If only there was a way to do it without having to speak to Norah.* Shaking his head, he punched Norah's number in his phone.

Norah answered, her voice still ice-cold. "Hello."

"Hey, can you put Pip on the phone?" It was a struggle to keep his tone civil.

After a second, he heard, "Hi, D-D-Daddy. I miss you. We're having a Thanksgiving feast at school in t-two weeks. Will you be b-b-back by then?"

"Of course I will, baby girl. I'll be home on Wednesday. Two sleeps." *Yeah, I'll be home, but where will she be?* Her stutter broke his heart. It seemed worse over the phone.

"I love you, D-D-Daddy."

"I love you more."

Norah took the phone back, which forced him to talk to her. She gave him the details about the feast, which would be the day before the Thanksgiving break. Then she asked, "How late were you?" Sam could hear the sarcasm dripping from her words.

"I arrived on time for the sessions that mattered."

"That's a surprise. I guess there's a first time for everything." Sam heard the stove's timer going off. "Our dinner is ready. I need to go." And with that, Norah ended the call.

Sam sat on the bed, holding his head in his hands. He couldn't do this any longer. He loved Norah, but the tension over the last few years had been slowly eroding that love. The morning's announcement, combined with the sarcastic jab she just hurled at him, was the final straw. He didn't want to be part of a failed relationship and especially didn't want to be separated from Piper for part of every week, but he'd reached his end.

Sam picked up his phone. The conversation lasted longer than he planned, and he still needed to shower. He shot Quinn a text to let her know about the delay. After showering, he put on jeans, a collared shirt, and a navy fleece vest, hoping the clothes were appropriate.

He sat back down on the bed for a minute, his thoughts going back to Norah. *I've never been alone. This is going to be difficult, but it can't be any worse than the turmoil I've been in. Not just me—it's been detrimental for all three of us.*

The memory of the concierge flitted into his mind, and Sam snorted. *I guess there will be women available if I want one. Which I don't. All I want to do now is catch up with Quinn. I'll figure the rest out later.*

His stomach was doing jumping jacks at the prospect of sitting down with Quinn. He had been heartlessly cruel to her at the end of their relationship, so he wasn't sure what her side of the conversation would be like. It didn't matter. There were things she needed to know.

Reminding himself that it was simply dinner with a friend, he took some deep breaths and walked out of his room. *I deserve whatever she says to me.*

Chapter 4
A Handsome Man at the Bar

Quinn

QUINN HAD SCARCELY SAID a word, not trusting her voice. *Jesus, you're acting like you did when you were a kid!* Needing a minute to think, and to get out of the throng of people, Quinn made her way to the elevator and pushed the button for her floor. She hurried to her room, letting herself in, then tossing her phone on the bed.

She walked to the window, where the view of the city skyline brought her a sense of peace. Absentmindedly drawing her hair into a bun, she took several deep breaths. *Did I really agree to have dinner with Sam Carpenter?*

It was only a meal, just two friends sharing a meal. Because they had been great friends and losing his friendship had left a huge hole in her life.

Quinn continued to take deep breaths to quiet her churning stomach while alternatives to the dinner floated through her mind. Not showing up—that was a possibility, but not her style. She honored her commitments, and her nod at his suggestion to meet in the lobby and giving him her number probably counted as a commitment.

Her cell signaled an incoming text, making her jump, and she walked back to the bed, eyeing the phone nervously. *Surely it's not him.* She reached for the phone as if it would give her an electric shock.

No, thank God. It's Angie asking where I am. Damn, we'd talked about having lunch together. Sam's got me all off-kilter. Quinn texted that she'd gone back to her room and was going to skip lunch.

Angie: You okay, girlfriend?

Quinn: Yeah, I'll munch on snacks in my room and meet you at the workshop.

Quinn and Angie had met two years earlier on the first day of a weekend class for their advanced nursing degree program. It was an online program, but once a month, the students traveled to Maine for in-person classes. Quinn had arrived at the class-room early to have her choice of seats and to avoid unwanted attention, and she was surprised to find someone else—Angie—had arrived at the classroom even before her.

As their friendship blossomed, a competition developed between them to be first to the classroom and first in grades. They had little in common outside of school. At twenty-nine, Quinn was single and living on her own in rural New Hampshire. Angie lived in New York City and was older, married, and had three kids who pulled her in a dozen different directions. The schoolwork was hard, but they loved the nights they spent discussing their classes, their jobs, and their lives over a bottle of wine.

Quinn went to the bathroom to splash some water on her face. She returned to the window, staring out at the city while she ate a granola bar. She checked the schedule for the afternoon. The workshop would end at four, which would give her time to transcribe her notes and hit the pool for a few laps. Swimming always cleared her mind and would relax her before dinner.

Quinn was still in her room when another text from Angie arrived.

Angie: Where are you?

Quinn: On my way, save me a seat.

She hurried downstairs and entered the lecture hall in the middle of a crowd of people. She searched for Angie and found her in the back row. They hugged like old friends who hadn't seen each other in months, even though it had only been three weeks since they were last together in Maine.

They both started talking at the same time. Angie said, "I didn't make it to the first session this morning because I started later than I had planned. I arrived five minutes into the keynote speaker. That was such an impressive speech! Topical but funny at the same time."

Quinn admitted, "I didn't hear a thing that was said. Someone I knew in high school sat next to me, and it unleashed a torrent of memories. We're going to have dinner tonight to catch up."

Angie raised her eyebrows. "Hey, girl, I need details," but at the same moment, the instructor took the podium and started speaking.

Quinn put her finger to her lips then sent a text.

> *Quinn: I'll tell you the complete story tomorrow at dinner.*

Determined to focus on the speaker, Quinn took her iPad from her bag and opened her note-taking app. The hospital paid for her to attend the conference, and she needed to come back with some new ideas. The nurse who'd had the position before her had done so little that Quinn didn't even know there *was* a wellness coordinator until the notice about an opening was posted. She was determined to do better.

The afternoon session focused on creating a welcoming workplace, which Quinn knew was an issue for her floor. Veteran staff often regarded new nurses or aids with suspicion, and the pace was so hectic that there was never time to welcome and orient newcomers. It had taken her more than six months to be accepted by the staff. The speaker covered mentors and how to select good ones from the existing staff. The strategies offered impressed Quinn.

Thank God my emotions stopped spiraling, and I paid better attention than I did this morning.

The speaker opted to skip the break and finish earlier, and Quinn was delighted to have extra free time.

Angie stretched. "I'm going to take a nap. It was a hectic morning, and I want to take advantage of being in a hotel room by myself. Lord knows I never get to nap at home." She grinned. "And I know you're going to transcribe your notes."

Quinn's routine with her notes was legendary among their classmates. She laughed. "When I'm done with my obsessive-compulsive transcription of notes from my iPad to my laptop, I'm going to the pool to swim some laps."

Thirty minutes later, notes complete, Quinn changed into her bathing suit and headed to the pool, which was empty. Pulling her hair into a ponytail, she jumped into the lane reserved for laps. Her arms sliced cleanly through the water for two laps each of the backstroke, butterfly, and breaststroke. She treaded water for a couple of minutes and repeated the six laps.

Swimming had been an integral part of Quinn's life since childhood. She'd been on the swim team in high school but had given it up in college. Four years ago, to become healthier, she'd returned to swimming regularly. The steady rhythm of her arms moving through the water always calmed her, no matter what turmoil was going on in her life.

With the laps completed, she flipped over to her back and floated lazily for a few minutes before climbing out and sinking into the bubbles of the hot tub.

She heard someone else climbing in and slowly opened her eyes. Delighted, she exclaimed, "Angie! I didn't expect to see you."

"Hey, you said *pool*, and that pushed away all thoughts of a nap." She sat across from Quinn, letting the jets massage her neck. "This is amazing. I like that retractable glass roof. I'd love to be here during a snowstorm, watching fat, fluffy snowflakes fall."

"I've done that, and it's awesome."

They sat silently for a few minutes until Quinn noticed the time. "Oh man, I need to get ready for that dinner I told you about. Walk back to my room with me."

Earlier, Quinn had pulled clothes out of her suitcase trying to decide what to wear. When she and Angie entered her room, Angie's eyes opened wide as she saw the pile of clothes on the bed. "How long are you planning to be here?"

"I know, I know. I'll never be accused of under packing. But you never know what opportunity might come along." *Like an unexpected dinner with my high school sweetheart.* "I'm going to take a quick shower. See what you think would work."

Returning a few minutes later wrapped in a towel, Quinn saw that Angie had tried to make some order out of the mounds of clothes. Picking up a couple of items, Quinn said, "I was thinking either this sweater with jeans or this dress."

"Wear the purple sweater and skinny jeans with silver jewelry and your black boots," Angie advised. "Save the dress for our dinner tomorrow night. I'm treating you to celebrate your new position at the hospital."

Quinn protested, but Angie would hear none of it.

"Now, I need to leave. I'm meeting a classmate from college, remember?" Angie gave her a quick hug. "Have fun tonight. I have a feeling this is more than just someone you knew in high school. I expect all the details tomorrow."

Quinn left her hair down and applied some makeup. Not an excessive amount, but enough to make her feel confident. Checking herself out in the full-length mirror, she was pleased with her appearance. She took a deep breath and thought, *Here goes nothing,* then made her way to the elevator.

Quinn stepped off the elevator into the large lobby, teeming with people. They had not agreed on a specific location, and she realized that was a mistake. Then her phone chimed.

That narrowed things down, and she made her way to the lounge, which was buzzing with activity. Well-dressed men and women lined the bar, unwinding after their workday. A grin crossed her face as she saw a woman wearing a pair of high heels that were far out of her price range. *I know from window-shopping those shoes cost more than I make in a month.*

This is so different from home. In New Hampshire or Vermont, the required attire was flannel and jeans worn with sneakers or work boots. *What a difference a hundred miles makes.*

The bartender was efficiently dispensing drinks, and as he walked back from the end of the bar, he pulled out a bottle of top-shelf Irish whiskey. "Get you another, Cade?" A handsome man pushed his glass forward for the refill.

Oh my. I don't see men who look like that very often. His back was to her, but his face was reflected in the mirror behind the liquor bottles. Dark, curly hair lapped over the collar of his white shirt. And his long legs were encased in well-tailored black pants. While he was talking animatedly with the bartender, he reached up to loosen his tie, which Quinn noticed enhanced the blue of his eyes. There was a lanyard beside his glass that matched hers.

The two men laughed at something, and Cade downed the whiskey before fist-bumping the bartender and picking up the lanyard. "I need to head out. I'm way beyond the one drink I intended to have."

As he turned to leave, Quinn glanced down, not wanting to be caught staring. When she raised her eyes, he'd turned toward the exit, but Quinn felt his eyes linger on her for a moment before he walked away. Butterflies invaded her stomach. *Damn! What are the chances he lives near me? Slim to none. I might break my moratorium on dating for someone like that.*

Chapter 5
Dinner

Quinn

S AM APPROACHED, AND Q UINN had only a second to prepare herself before he gathered her into a brief hug.

"Have you gotten taller?" he asked.

She pointed to the heels on her boots and said, "I wish."

"You look pretty. We have a reservation at a seafood place. That used to be your favorite—is it still?"

"Yes." It touched her that he remembered, but her mind was overcome with thoughts about how awkward she felt being with him.

The restaurant was located close to the hotel, and neither of them spoke on the short walk. Quinn was uncomfortable with the silence, feeling like she should make conversation but unable to come up with one thing to say. *God, why did I agree to have dinner with him? This is such a mistake.*

The host led them to a table in a back corner of the restaurant, away from the noisy hubbub at the front, and a server appeared to take their drink orders. Quinn ordered a margarita, and Sam selected a Fiddlehead IPA, saying, "I like to stay true to Vermont brewers."

Quinn studied the menu, praying the drinks would arrive quickly. She needed the relaxation alcohol always brought her, as she was completely tongue-tied.

I've never had alcohol with Sam. How is that going to be? When they'd broken up, she had recently turned nineteen, and he'd only been twenty-one for a couple of months. The underage drinking that plagued many high school students had never appealed to her, and he'd had no interest in drinking, which Quinn knew stemmed from watching his father drink way too much, way too often.

The server returned to take their orders, and as Quinn ordered broiled salmon with rice pilaf she thought, *Damn, why did you come back without our drinks?*

Sam chose rib eye steak with fries. When the server left, he said, "You just had a birthday, didn't you?" They were the first words he had said to her since they met in the lobby. He smiled and added, "Twenty-nine."

"Don't remind me. Thirty next year. I'm surprised you remember."

"I remember a lot. How was your afternoon workshop?"

"It was good, and I already have ideas I'll work on im-plementing." She gazed at him, realizing he was nervous too. "Where are you working and living? I know you have a daughter, but that's about all the hometown rumor mill has told me."

A chuckle escaped his mouth. "The gossip mongers aren't doing their job. I live in Thetford, and I'm a project planner for an economic development group based there."

Quinn realized his home was only about twenty miles from her. What were the odds?

He laughed again, saying, "It sounds far removed from my degree in architecture, but I took courses in project management, so there is some relevancy. I know you're a registered nurse, but where are you working? The last I heard, you were in Washington state."

"I've been at Dartmouth Hitchcock for two years, after a year in Virginia and three years in Seattle."

Sam's head tilted. "I'm surprised. I didn't think you'd ever come back to New England once you escaped."

She picked up her water glass and gazed at it. "I hadn't planned on it, but Dartmouth made an offer I couldn't refuse. More money, down payment on housing, and tuition reim-bursement. I'm doing an online program for my master's degree. I'm exceptionally happy there." She raised her eyes to meet his and smiled.

"I'm working on a master's degree in project management."

Quinn raised her eyebrows in surprise at that.

"Yeah, it surprised me too," he said. "I never envisioned getting an advanced degree."

Their drinks arrived, and Sam raised his. "To old friends."

She raised her glass and tapped Sam's lightly before taking a swallow. The warmth traveled down her throat into her belly, and she knew relaxation would follow.

As her tension lessened, Quinn said, "You don't live far from me. I'm surprised we've never run into each other. Do you shop in West Leb?"

"I don't shop much. Norah works in Montpelier and shops there." Sam's face flushed after he mentioned his significant other.

Okay, so her name's Norah. Cue the awkward pause.

The server arrived with their meals, which provided a distraction. The teriyaki sauce on the salmon exploded on her taste buds. "Mm-mmm. This is delicious. How's yours?"

"It's good."

"Good."

There was a long moment of silence where they both concentrated on their food. Finally, Sam put his fork down and said, "I went for a run this afternoon and saw these bronze ducklings in Boston Common. They're cool. There were kids sitting on them and having their pictures taken. My daughter would love to see those."

Her mouth curled up in a smirk. "Don't let a true Bostonian hear you say they're in the Common. They're actually in the

Public Garden. It can be difficult to know where the Garden begins and the Common ends. And yes, I've seen them. If the sports teams make the playoffs, they dress them in sports garb like Red Sox caps or Bruins jerseys." She paused. "Have you been to Boston before?"

"This is my first time. When I was planning the trip, I knew there was someone in my past who'd raved about Boston. I'm thinking it was you."

"Guilty as charged. I love it here." Quinn smiled. "What's your daughter's name?"

Sam reached for his phone as he answered. "It's Piper, also known as Pip. Would you like to see a picture?"

"I would."

Sam scrolled through pictures on his phone, and when he finally handed it to her, Quinn saw a young girl with long brown hair and Sam's blue eyes.

"I see your eyes! How old is she?"

"Just turned six. Totally a combination of Norah and me, but there are people who see more of me in her. She's super intelligent. She was reading before starting kindergarten." Sam's eyes glowed as he talked about her.

"I'm surprised you only have one. I always pictured you with at least a couple of kids."

Sam stared down at his plate. "We decided it would be irresponsible to bring more than one child into the world."

His words stunned Quinn. And his tone was robotic, with none of the warmth he'd had seconds earlier talking about Piper. Global thinking was never his thing, which added to her shock.

Sam met her eyes again. "What about you? Kids? Are you involved with anyone?"

"No kids, no involvements. I know it sounds lame, but I've focused on work and school since I moved back here. Are you and Norah married?" His ring finger was bare, but she knew that meant nothing. "I always pictured you married too."

"No. We don't need a piece of paper to legitimize our relationship," Sam responded, again without looking at her and in that robotic tone.

Quinn wondered if he was embarrassed.

They fell into an awkward silence while both of them finished their meals.

Sam laid his fork down and finally spoke again. "Do you still ski?"

"A few times a year. My parents have a condo on the mountain that I can use whenever I want since they spend the winters in Florida."

"Oh nice. I remember your mom didn't like the cold. What else do you do for fun?"

"I run a little, and I like to cook. I have friends I get together with once a month to prepare an elaborate meal. We eat way too much and share too many bottles of wine, but it's fun." They had both ordered second drinks, and she took a swallow of hers. "Obviously, you're still running. Do you race?"

"In my dreams I do, but honestly, it's been a couple of years. I'd like to run a marathon, but I struggle to find the time to do the training."

"How about skiing?" He had been a strong skier when they were on the team together.

"No, I haven't skied in years."

They sat in silence again as they finished their drinks.

Quinn took a deep breath. *We've run out of things to say.* "This is awkward, huh?"

Sam snorted. "A little. I don't want it to be. I have such warm memories of you and have always wondered where life had taken you."

His memories are drastically different from mine. Those words did not align at all with the texts he had sent after the fight that ended their relationship. "I wouldn't blame you if you hated me. I was shitty to you after I left for college. And at some other times too."

"We both did some shitty things, especially at the end," he said. "But once I moved beyond being mad and hurt, what I remembered were the good times."

Quinn was touched. But she suspected Sam had recovered from their breakup quickly, maybe because he moved directly from her to another relationship. For Quinn, many months had gone by with her clinging to the hope that they would reconcile.

When the reconciliation didn't happen, what finally enabled her to move on was identifying all the things that were wrong with the relationship. She'd reached a point where she actively disliked Sam and tried not to wonder how he was or what he was doing.

But here they were, having dinner, and Sam was acting all warm and considerate. It felt like it had that first year.

The server brought the check, and Quinn took out her wallet to pay her share, but Sam beat her to it. As weird as it was being with Sam, she wasn't ready for the evening to end. "Did you know there are stores adjoining the hotel and an elevated walkway across the road leading to an upscale shopping area?"

He shook his head.

"We could walk around. You can find something to bring back for Norah and Piper." Norah's name flowed off her lips easily, surprising her. *Maybe I am totally beyond where Sam being firmly entrenched in a relationship can wound me. This is good.*

Sam agreed, and as they walked, he said, "You mentioned running earlier. I thought you hated running. I remember you doing anything to get out of it during the preseason for the ski team." His shoulder nudged hers. "When did that change?"

"Preseason was the worst. Especially with the captain being such a drill sergeant!" She nudged him back before getting more serious. "I slipped into a bad headspace in Seattle and spent far too much time lying on my bed watching Netflix. When I finally decided I had to turn things around, I started running and hiking. I also started swimming again."

"It must be working because you look great. Do you feel better mentally too?"

"Yeah, I'm much better since I came back to the northeast."

They stepped into a bookstore, and while he was searching for a book Piper would like, he asked her about hiking. She told him her favorite spots.

He nodded. "I have a friend who is into hiking, and we go exploring in the White Mountains." He found a book about Boston and a sweatshirt for Piper but ignored the items Quinn pointed out for Norah.

When he started yawning, Quinn suggested they head back to the hotel.

Sam

They walked past the lobby bar, and Sam paused. *I still need to tell her about Norah.*

"Hey, Quinn, let's have a nightcap." He walked toward an empty table. Quinn followed, and he pulled a chair out for her. "The server seems busy, so I'm going to order at the bar. I'm getting a bourbon on the rocks. Should I get two?"

"No, I'll have a tequila shot."

While Sam was at the bar, Quinn must have pulled out her phone to check her email, because when he returned, she said,

"The presenter for my morning session is sick, so health care and contractors are going to be combined. Is that your group?"

"It is. So maybe we'll see each other in the morning."

The server approached their table, placing the tumbler of bourbon in front of Sam. With a flourish, he gave Quinn a shot glass of tequila, a wedge of lime, and a saltshaker.

Quinn picked up the shaker, and Sam leaned back in his chair to watch with a wide grin. She smiled then sprinkled the salt on her hand, licked it off, knocked back the tequila, and picked up the lime wedge.

As she sucked on it, Sam said, "You've learned to drink."

Quinn chuckled. "I have, and I like tequila."

Sam took a sip of his bourbon. "Do you want another?"

"No, one is plenty."

Sam glanced around the bar. *Tell her. Tell her.* He couldn't stop that thought from reverberating in his brain. "This is some different from home."

Quinn nodded. "I had the same thought while I was waiting for you. But I had my share of big cities before I returned to New England. You haven't?"

"Not really. Norah's family lives in Connecticut, and we visit them and have gone to a few concerts in Hartford. We go to Maine every summer."

"Old Orchard Beach?" When Sam nodded, Quinn smiled. "I've been to Hampton Beach in New Hampshire but haven't made it back to the Maine beaches yet. I loved the time we spent there. Do you remember that sand dollar you found?"

"Yeah. Do you still have it?" He swallowed the last bit of bourbon and shook the glass, rattling the ice.

Quinn swiveled her head away. "I doubt it. Between all the moves I made and my parents moving to a different house, I think it was lost in the shuffle." She shook her head and sighed. "I don't know about you, but I'm ready to call it a night."

Probably a good idea. Because obviously I'm not going to tell her about Norah leaving.

As they walked toward the elevator, Sam said, "Thanks for helping me pick something out for Piper."

"I'm always up to go shopping."

When the doors opened on Sam's floor, he gave Quinn a quick hug and headed to his room. Once inside, he walked over to the window. The city lights provided a different view than at home, where the only light at night came from the stars and the moon.

His mind drifted back to dinner with Quinn. *She really got herself together. The shy teenager I was in love with has completely disappeared. I'm happy for her.*

Dammit, I should have told Quinn that Norah was moving out. I thought I'd be able to get the words out. "Norah and I have split up." Simple. But no. I'm such a wimp. I'm glad I'm having lunch with Jesse tomorrow.

Exhausted, Sam pulled his clothes off and crawled under the covers, where he fell asleep thinking about how much his life was about to change

Chapter 6
Quinn Snoops

Quinn

QUINN DRIFTED AWAKE WITH a smile on her face and reached across the bed for Sam, but her hands came up empty. A long-ago trip that Sam made to see her when she was dying of loneliness after two weeks at college had invaded her subconscious while she was sleeping. The sweet memories had made for a wonderful dream—but realization hit that it was all over.

Her desire had always been to attend a school far away from rural Vermont, and not even her relationship with Sam had derailed that. She had chosen a college in Virginia, over ten hours away. They had pledged to remain true to each other, working out all the ways they would stay in touch and how often they would see each other.

However, she had not anticipated the level of homesickness that would overtake her in Virginia, despite spending hours on the phone talking to Sam. After a two-hour call in which all

Quinn did was sob, Sam had jumped in his car and driven all night to visit her. He spent several days with her, and despite the way their relationship imploded a few weeks later, it still had a place in her heart as the most romantic thing that had ever happened to her.

Quinn lay in bed for a few more minutes, thinking about that visit from Sam and hoping to get back to sleep and back to the dream. Frustrated, she finally rolled over to check the time. *Five thirty. Damn. I might as well get up.*

Reluctantly, Quinn climbed out of bed and searched for her running clothes. She could do three miles and still be ready on time for the morning session.

As she tied her shoes, she remembered how she had slumped against the elevator wall the second the doors slid shut behind Sam the night before. She'd been relieved to survive dinner with Sam Carpenter. The evening had actually gone better than Quinn expected. *Until Sam asked if I still had that damn sand dollar. Why did I bring it up?*

Quinn knew exactly what had happened to the sand dollar. The night Sam broke up with her, after her tears had finally stopped flowing, she'd placed it on the floor and brought her foot down on it with all the fury in her body. It was smashed to bits, exactly like their relationship.

As she ran, Boston Common and the Public Garden unwound under her feet, and memories of trips with her parents for weekend getaways came back. They'd gone to Red Sox games and museums, and a smile crossed her face as she remembered riding on the swan boats and her delight in taking an elevator to the observation deck on the top floor of a skyscraper.

That must be where my fascination with the city skyline was born. Boston was one of her favorite cities, even if it didn't have the polish of Seattle or Richmond. It was old and laden with history. The traffic was notoriously bad, and the vibe could be gritty, but that didn't matter to her. She was happy to be running along the streets, and it felt good to watch the city waking up.

The night before, with Sam, had involved awkward moments, but it had been better than she anticipated. She was touched by the things that he remembered—her birthday, her love of seafood, their day at the beach. And that dream. It all reminded her of the tender and kind young man she had been with for two years. Her anger toward him was fading, and in the long run, that would be good for her mental health.

His responses to her questions about why he didn't have more than one child and if he was married still troubled her. His words were not the language the old Sam would have used. *Was he parroting Norah's words? Is she the driver of the relationship?*

She shook her head. *It doesn't matter.*

Quinn put Sam out of her mind and focused on enjoying the run. It was pleasant, with the streets relatively empty and the air cool. After three miles, footsteps came pounding up the pavement behind her. That always gave her pause; she'd been fortunate to avoid being harassed but was always on guard. She moved to the right to let the runner pass, but the steps slowed, and someone pulled up beside her.

Before she turned her head, instinct told her it was Sam. "Hey." Her breath was coming hard.

"Hey, yourself," Sam panted. "I didn't expect to see you out here."

"I was awake and figured I had time to get a three-mile run in." Checking her watch, she added, "And I'm there, so I'm going to walk the rest of the way back to the hotel as a cooldown. Don't let me hold you up."

"My plan was for five, and I'm right there, so I'll walk with you if that's okay."

She nodded and worked on catching her breath.

They reached the hotel still slightly winded, and Sam leaned against the brick planter surrounding the hotel before bending down with his hands on his knees. "This was great. I seldom get to run like this in the morning."

Quinn enjoyed the fall decor as she stretched while her breathing returned to normal. Brightly colored fall mums filled the planter, and hay bales, cornstalks, and pumpkins surrounded the hotel entrance. She ran her hand through her hair and shook her head. "I am so hot and sweaty. I need a shower." She turned toward the entrance to the hotel.

"Hey, Quinn," Sam called. "Your stride was a lot better this morning than it used to be on those preseason runs." He held up his hand to high-five her.

She smirked. "Thanks, captain." Her hand slapped his as she walked past.

After a shower, Quinn found Auditorium K, and even with her run, there were only a few people as early as she was. There was a breakfast buffet with pastries, fruit, and coffee. Grabbing a Danish, an orange for later, and a cup of coffee, she found a seat in the middle of the auditorium and immediately pulled her hair into a ponytail. *Damn, I'm still hot.*

Everything was more familiar now, so Quinn was more comfortable than she had been the day before. A text from Angie popped up while she was scrolling.

> Angie: Negotiating a truce from afar. I don't know why these kids don't understand that their father is right there and I'm 200 miles away. So I'll be late. Don't save me a spot, I'll sit wherever.

Quinn shook her head. *Man, those kids give her a run for her money.*

Sam walked in, and she watched him search the room. *He's looking for me. Not sure how I feel about that. Yup, here he comes.*

He made his way to her row, cocking his head at her as if to ask if the seat was available, and she patted the seat cushion to show him it was empty.

"You're a little earlier than yesterday," she said.

He was chewing a bite of his donut and had to swallow before he could speak. "Sorry, I'm starving. Yes. Thankfully, I didn't have to battle the traffic today."

The speaker started promptly at nine by apologizing for the change in location and explaining that the presenter for the health group had a sick child. The session provided great information, and Quinn stayed busy taking notes even though she knew she would have access to the PowerPoint. She glanced over at Sam and saw that his approach was different and did not include note-taking. *Just like high school.* Otherwise, her focus remained on the speaker until there was a break at midmorning.

Sam rose to go to the bathroom. "I'm going to get a second cup of coffee. Can I get you one? Still one sugar and a little cream?"

"I'd love a second cup." Quinn stood to stretch her legs and started looking around the room. She finally spotted Angie in the front row, scrolling on her phone. Standing next to her, also studying the room, was an exceptionally handsome man with curly black hair and deep-blue eyes. His white shirt was paired with a blue patterned tie and a gray V-neck sweater. He caught her staring at him and smiled.

She smiled back and then turned away. It was embarrassing to get caught like that. Her ogling was usually more discrete, and he was ogle-worthy. *I think that's the same guy I saw at the bar. Lucky Angie, getting to sit next to him.* Angie caught her eye, and Quinn waved in response.

Quinn settled back for the rest of the morning and noticed that Sam had left a spiral-bound notebook on his seat. *Was he taking notes after all?* Leaning over to get a closer peek, she saw a drawing of a ranch house. She picked it up to examine it more closely. The house was surrounded by an elaborate landscaping scheme with each bush and flower labeled in careful block printing.

When they were younger, Sam had always been drawing. When he was in college and came to her house on the weekends, almost the first thing he would do was share his sketches with her. He'd always said academics hadn't been his thing, and she thought about how she used to tell him that he'd get better grades if he took notes rather than doodling all the time. *God, I was such a nag. He actually did well, considering how many different directions his mind wandered.*

Sam returned with two cups of coffee while Quinn was still holding the notebook. She blushed. "You caught me. I'm sorry. I shouldn't be nosing around your stuff. I was curious."

Sam smiled. "It's okay. It's just a drawing, not my private diary."

"Still, I'm embarrassed. Is it a work project?"

"No, it's my house. I want to work on the landscaping next summer, and I'm trying to decide on the plants."

"How long have you lived there?"

"I... We bought it when Piper was a baby."

"It's not the Craftsman style we used to talk about living in."

Sam laughed. "That's for sure. This fit our budget and needed a ton of work. I finally finished all that, and now it's time for the outside. How about you? What's your home like?"

"I bought a townhouse in Hanover soon after I started at Dartmouth." She laughed. "Also not a Craftsman, but like you, I got what I could afford. It does have a fireplace though."

"Ah yes, I remember a fireplace was important. I also have one."

The next speaker strode to the lectern, and they settled in for the rest of the morning session. Once the speaker finished, they started making their way to the door, but Sam seemed to be searching for someone.

"I'm meeting someone for lunch, but I'm not sure if he was in this session or a different one," he explained.

As they fought their way through the crush of people, he was struggling to get his phone out of his pocket. When they finally reached the hallway, Quinn took a deep breath and started laughing. "Dang, I didn't know if we'd make it out alive!"

Sam's laughter joined hers. As he was checking his phone, a man grabbed his arm and said, "You need to watch where you are walking."

Sam jerked his head up. "Jesse! How are you, man?" They both smiled as they exchanged a brief bro hug. They chatted for a minute, then Jesse glanced at Quinn, who was standing awkwardly at Sam's side, waiting for a break in their conversation so she could excuse herself.

She offered her hand and said, "Quinn Michaels. So nice of Sam to introduce us."

Jesse glanced at Sam quizzically then offered his hand. "Jesse Ortega. Nice to meet you."

"Quinn's a friend from high school," Sam stammered, his face bright red.

Jesse raised his eyebrows, still gazing curiously at both of them.

Something was going on, and it didn't make sense to Quinn. But Angie was walking toward them, giving her an excuse to take her leave.

Quinn and Angie spent time touring the vendor booths scattered over the second floor. After seeing them all, they grabbed a to-go lunch and headed toward the auditorium. As they ate, Quinn talked about her final class project, and Angie briefly outlined her own.

"I'm worried about the next few weeks, with course work, the job, and Thanksgiving," Quinn admitted.

Angie nodded. "It's going to be hell."

"And I don't have kids like you do."

Angie took a call from her husband, and while she was talking, Quinn picked up the program they had received at registration. When she was walking away from Sam, she'd heard him saying something to his friend, Jesse, about Jesse's presentation. Turning the pages, she perused the presenters until she found Jesse's photo and biography. He appeared more polished in the photo than he had in the hallway, an attractive Latino with dark hair and warm brown eyes. It startled Quinn to read in the bio that Jesse had a PhD. "Whoa!" *That's certainly not the crowd Sam used to hang out in.*

Angie finished on the phone and peered over at what Quinn was reading. "Someone you know?"

"I met him at the end of the last session. He's a friend of the person I knew in high school."

Chapter 7
Not the Same Boy

Sam

ONCE QUINN LEFT, SAM started moving. "We should get to lunch. I know you're doing one of the first presentations this afternoon."

As they walked, Jesse interrogated him. "Quinn? As in the girlfriend from high school? How did that happen? The last thing you told me was about Norah moving out."

Sam's phone buzzed with a message from Quinn.

> Quinn: What was that all about? Who is Jesse, and why did he act like he knew me? Why were you blushing? Are you embarrassed to be seen with me?

"Whoa, whoa, whoa, so many questions!" he said to Jesse. "I'll explain when we have our food."

> Sam: He's a friend. Can we get together later, and I'll tell you about him?

It took Quinn several minutes to reply

Quinn: I'm having dinner with my friend Angie.

Sam: Meet for a drink after?

Her lack of an answer left Sam hanging.

Sam and Jesse went through the buffet set up for the conference, filling their plates, then they found a table. Before taking a bite of his sandwich, Jesse said, "All right. So how did you go from the devastated message I received Monday morning about Norah leaving to laughing with your high school girlfriend?"

Sam explained how he had arrived late on Monday, ended up sitting next to Quinn, and they had gone out to dinner to catch up. And come across each other while running in the morning. And sat together for the morning session.

Jesse shook his head. "Now you're fine with the whole Norah thing? Because honestly, this feels like what you've done in the past. Having someone ready to move on with."

"No, it's not like that. Quinn was a good friend, an integral part of how I became who I am. You know that. We've talked about it several times." Sam took a bite of his sandwich and washed it down with a drink of water. "Was I supposed to act like I didn't know her? I always wondered where life had taken her." He drummed his fingers on the table. "You know, more than anyone, I've always been curious."

"Okay, I'll give you that."

Sam nodded then shared his realization from the night before. "I'm done with Norah."

Jesse's eyes opened wide, and he cocked his head. "Because of Quinn?"

Sam shook his head. "No. No. I reached that decision before Quinn and I went to dinner. You should have heard the malice in Norah's voice yesterday morning and when I called to talk to Pip last night. It made me realize there's nothing left. I can't live with being treated that way any longer. And that's not like Norah, being so angry and mean all the time. At least, it's not the Norah I fell in love with eight years ago." He sighed. "We're not good for each other. There may have been love between us, but there's no *like* left."

Jesse put his sandwich down. "For what it's worth, I've been wondering how long it was going to take you to come to that conclusion. But are you sure Quinn's not playing a part in it?"

Sam finished his sandwich. "Honestly? I'm not sure of much."

"Walk with me to the auditorium." As they left the dining room, Jesse asked, "Did you tell Quinn about Norah moving out?"

"No," Sam admitted sheepishly, "I kind of implied that everything was good between us."

Jesse shook his head. "I thought you were going to stop doing that!" They had talked extensively about Sam's tendency to withhold difficult information. "Did you at least apologize for the way you ended things? You've told me more than once how much you regret that."

Chagrined, Sam said, "No."

"Are you going to see her again?"

"I'd like to, but we're only here until tomorrow. It was comfortable talking with her—well, that is, after the awkwardness passed. I'm truly not looking for someone to move on with, but it was nice to spend time with someone who didn't seem to judge me. Especially since judgment is all I get from Norah these days."

"You've told me how much you regret the lack of candor between the two of you when things ended. This could be your chance to finally stop beating yourself up over that."

"Is this a counseling session?" Sam grinned. Jesse had a degree in psychology, and Sam often told him he should be a therapist rather than a workforce consultant.

"Do you need one?"

"Probably."

Jesse smiled back. "We'd be digging a lot deeper if it was."

They arrived at the auditorium, where, with Sam's help, Jesse started setting up his presentation. People drifted in to take seats, but there were still several minutes before Jesse needed to start his talk.

"You've never been alone for an extended period of time, have you?" Jesse asked.

Sam shook his head. "Nope. Not excited about it either."

"What about Pip? You'll have her part of the time, won't you?"

"Of course!" Sam's face crumpled. "Norah mentioned setting up a visitation schedule as she was shoving me out the door. Do you think she's going to try cutting me out of Pip's life?"

Jesse shrugged. "That doesn't seem like something she'd do. She knows how close you and Piper are."

"I want her to spend half her time with me. It kills me to think about missing out on bedtime or her waking me up in the morning."

"I've got my schedule set up now so that I have Wednesday afternoons off. Why don't you plan on coming for dinner? Caitlin will be glad to see you, and the kids always love it when you visit. It'll give some structure to your life."

"Are you talking about every week?"

"Yeah, it'll give you and me a chance to talk like we used to back in the day when we shared an office."

Sam wanted to say yes, but... "That's your one free afternoon. I appreciate the offer, but I can't intrude like that."

"Caitlin and I talked about it after your call on Monday. I wouldn't have offered if we didn't want to do it. So when you can shake yourself loose from your office on Wednesday, head our way."

Sam smiled. "Thanks, man. I appreciate it."

They fist-bumped before Sam left and Jesse headed to the stage."

Quinn

Once the afternoon session ended, Quinn mentioned going for a swim, while Angie said she was going to try for the nap she had skipped the day before. They agreed to meet for dinner at the Cheesecake Factory.

Quinn put on her purple tank suit and made her way to the pool. After six laps, she took a break and soon heard the door open. Someone jumped into the pool and swam over to her. *Sam.*

"Got six more laps to swim." Her tone left no room for conversation as she began moving through the water again.

Sam tried to match her lap for lap, but he faltered after the fourth one. Hanging on the side of the pool, he watched her swim.

After the six laps, Quinn waved to him and said, "Join me in the hot tub." She toweled off her hair as she walked to the hot tub then sank into the bubbles with a sigh.

Sam did the same.

Finding a jet to massage her back, she asked, "Are you stalking me?" Her tone reflected a mixture of humor and irritation.

His face reddened. "I... No, of course not." When Quinn stared pointedly at him, he added, "Well, I thought you might be here."

She sighed. "Tell me about Jesse."

"What do you want to know?"

"Lots of things. I found him in the program. He has a PhD and is a presenter at this conference. Where did that friendship come from? It's a big change from the auto mechanics and loggers you used to hang out with. And what were the looks between the two of you? Why did he act like he knew me?"

"We shared an office at my first job. He was a valuable mentor for me." Sam moved around in the hot tub, seeming to want to get the jets to hit his neck much like she had, shifting his position and sinking deep into the water. "He started his own consulting firm about five years ago and travels all over New England, helping companies to function more efficiently. We became good friends before he left—he's the person I mentioned last night who likes to hike in the Whites. And one of his three kids is the same age as Piper, so we've done some family things together too. Truthfully, he's my best friend."

Sam stopped talking, and for a while the only sound came from the hot tub jets and the bubbles rising to the water's surface.

Then he said, "My circle of friends is different now, Quinn. The people I hung out with in high school were the ones I'd grown up with. My dad worked in a factory, my uncles did road construction—it was strictly a blue-collar existence. Your family was my first exposure to a different world. And I liked it. That was the life I wanted and went after."

Surprised, Quinn raised her hands out of the water. "Hey. It's not like my family was wealthy."

"Wealthier than mine was. I hope you don't think I'm the same boy I was when we met. I mean you're not the same shy little bird who fell into my arms on those stairs."

Quinn scoffed. "I was hardly a 'little' bird!"

"That was only an issue for you. I thought you were perfect." Sam waited a moment as if to emphasize his words, before he continued, "I left our dinner last night thinking about how much you had moved on from the shy teenager that you were. I hope you can see similar changes in me."

"Point taken. I need to stop thinking of you as the eighteen-year-old I had a crush on. We're both different people. But I still want to know about those looks between you and Jesse."

"It was probably that he realized you were my girlfriend from high school. We've talked about our dating histories, and I'm sure I mentioned you." He hesitated before continuing. "Can we get together for a drink after your dinner with your friend? I have some things I'd like to talk to you about."

Wariness must have clouded her eyes because he added, "We'll probably never see each other again after tonight. Unless I start shopping in West Leb and run into you at the grocery store." That signature grin flashed across his face.

Quinn found herself agreeing to meet him at the lobby bar.

Chapter 8
The Exit Strategy

Quinn

QUINN WAS EXCITED ABOUT dinner with Angie. She put on a long camel-colored skirt and an oatmeal-colored sweater with brown boots. The shop windows on her walk to the Cheesecake Factory were filled with displays of beautiful dresses, making her realize how enjoyable it was wearing pretty clothes every day. The thought of going back to scrubs next week was disheartening.

She needed this walk. The last twenty-four hours—running into Sam, having dinner with him, plus all the other encounters—had been weird and stressful, making her feel like she had to keep her guard up.

I wonder what he wants to talk about. This is probably when everything about how badly I hurt him at the end is going to come out.

Angie caught up with her before she arrived at the restaurant. As soon as they were seated, they ordered a bottle of wine and appetizers.

When the server left, Angie immediately said, "All right, tell me about the hottie you had dinner with last night, because he must be something special to get you this rattled."

Quinn sighed. "Forty-five minutes into the opening session, this guy took the empty seat next to me. I was pissed. I like having space between myself and strangers!"

Angie shook her head. "You know that's unrealistic at something like this."

"Yes, Mom. I know, but it doesn't mean I have to like it." Quinn rolled her eyes. The server brought their wine, and they shared a toast before Quinn continued. "So the lights came up, and it turned out the intruder was a guy I met on the first day of high school my sophomore year, when I fell down the stairs and landed in his arms. We ended up in the same health class and became friends even though he was a senior. We were on the ski team together and—"

Angie interrupted. "Wait, you've mentioned skiing, but you were good enough to be on the ski team?"

Indignant, Quinn mock-frowned. "Don't sound so surprised. I'm a fast skier, took some firsts in those high school meets."

"Did you have a crush on him?"

"Of course I did. I was going through an extremely awkward stage, and he was a cute senior, paying attention to me."

"But you never went out? You know, on a date?"

Quinn took another swallow of her wine and grinned at Angie. "I didn't say that. Shortly before he left for college, we went out to dinner. That was our first official date, and we became a couple. We were together for my last two years of high school. Every other weekend…"

"Back up. You were with someone for *two years*, and I know nothing about him?"

"It was a long time ago. I was a teenager! It's not relevant to who I am today."

"And yet, you accidentally run into him, and the next thing you know, he's taking you out to dinner. And you're skipping lunch. You never skip lunch! I want to know more."

Quinn gazed at the ceiling and nibbled on a fingernail before she turned back to Angie. "I was extremely introverted back then and…"

"Kind of like now?" Angie teased with a smile.

"Much worse. I was heavier than I am now, self-conscience about it, and afraid to talk to anyone. A total geek. I'd gone to a different school my freshman year, and you know how hard it is to break into friend circles that are already established. No one tried to get to know me. Except for Sam. Something clicked between us, and he became my best friend long before that first date. He filled all the gaps for me."

"What happened?"

"It ended after I left for college." She paused, seeing the questions in Angie's eyes. "I've never told anyone this. College was totally different from high school. We were all newcomers, and boys started paying attention to me. I was curious. Sam was the only guy I'd been out with, the only one I'd ever kissed and eventually slept with. I started being distant with him, not returning his calls or texts, and we finally agreed to take a break." Quinn rubbed her fingers on her wine glass before taking a sip. "I went to a movie with one of those boys, and we ended up back in my room. All I wanted was to get to know him, make out maybe. We ended up doing a lot more than that."

"Did he force you? God, that's so common on college campuses!"

Quinn could see the anger snapping in Angie's eyes. "I didn't consider it rape, if that's what you're asking, but I hadn't planned on having sex with him either. I was naive and trusting and let myself be carried away." She paused. "Sam had been so considerate, not pushing for anything that I wasn't ready to give, and I expected all guys would be like that. I realized what a huge mistake I'd made, and when we talked about ending the break, Sam asked what I'd done. I told him I'd been to some parties but nothing else. I was ashamed. I couldn't tell him that I'd had sex with someone."

Angie reached across the table and took Quinn's hand. "You were under no obligation to tell him."

"My mistake was telling a mutual friend who let it slip to Sam. I came home on break, thinking we were fine. Little did I know, we were far from it. He ended our relationship. That was the last time I talked to him until yesterday."

"Is he still in love with you?"

"Oh my God!" Quinn shook her head. "He's been in a relationship for several years and has a six-year-old daughter. He's definitely *not* still in love with me. Where do you get your imagination?"

"Romance novels. I live vicariously through them. So what was it like having dinner with him?"

"Tremendously awkward at first. I'm surprised that he's not married and that he only has one child, because the boy I went out with would be married and have two or three kids. We even considered ourselves engaged for a hot minute." She twirled her wine glass between her hands. "He gave me a kind of bogus reply when I asked about that. Something about one child being better for the planet and not needing a piece of paper to legitimize his relationship."

"Maybe things aren't good between him and his partner. Is there still a spark for you? Would you give him another shot?"

"No, but it's been... unnerving. For ten years, I concentrated on all his weaknesses to get over him and now here he is. He pointed out to me this afternoon that he's changed, but I still see a lot of the sweet boy I knew. However, I don't have any interest in going backward, even if he was available. And I wouldn't want to be his exit strategy."

"Exit strategy?"

Quinn sighed. "In every relationship Sam has had, when it's nearing the end, he starts a new one before totally extricating himself from the previous one. When we took that break, there was already someone waiting in the wings, and he ended up being with her for a couple of years."

Quinn paused. Had she really once hidden in her car to avoid Sam? It was two years after their breakup, and her friend Julie had just told her that he'd left Ginger, the woman who'd taken Quinn's place. She shoved the memory away, going back to her conversation with Angie.

"And when he broke up with that girl, he was already talking with the woman he's with now. It's a pattern." Quinn polished off a breadstick and poured a second glass of wine.

"How do you know all that?"

"We had mutual friends, and they were all too happy to keep me updated on what he was doing."

"Like the one who told him what you'd done."

Quinn nodded.

"You need new friends."

Quinn laughed. "I finally figured that out. It's why I have you and my tribe in New Hampshire."

"But I've known you two years, and I don't think you've even been on a date. I hate to see you alone."

"It's my choice. I've explained how much I like my solitary life. I haven't told you much about my dating history because it's so dismal. And now, let's talk about something else, like our final projects or holiday plans. Anything but my nonexistent love life!"

They did. Quinn and Angie knew they would see each other the next morning but not again until January, so they discussed the holidays and the papers they needed to finish before the end of the semester.

Finally, Angie pushed her chair back. "I'd love to sit here and drink wine all night, but I promised to call the family at seven thirty."

Quinn hesitated before standing. "Sam wants me to meet him for a drink."

Angie gave her a quizzical smile.

"I'm nervous," Quinn confessed. "Our relationship ended badly, and I'm afraid he wants to rehash something. I don't want to hear it all from him again."

Angie gave her a hug. "Most endings are bad, but we all get over them. You'll be okay. See you in the morning."

Chapter 9
Sam's Confessions

Sam

SAM ARRIVED AT THE bar early and sat at the same table where they'd had the nightcap. He wanted to eat and have at least one beer before Quinn arrived. He was nervous about being open and honest with her. While he knew he was not inherently dishonest, he did have a tendency to avoid uncomfortable topics.

Two bites of his burger remained when his phone pinged with a text. He was afraid it was Quinn backing out on him, but relief flowed through him when he realized it was from his boss.

> John: Got you into that conference at Harvard on Thursday and Friday. I've extended your room reservation for two more nights. You'll have to take a rideshare over to Cambridge. I've emailed the agenda, etc. Enjoy a couple more nights in the big city!

This news surprised Sam. They had discussed the Harvard conference, but when he tried to register for it, it was full. He had put his name on a waiting list but hadn't expected anything to come from it.

Two more nights before I must face an empty house. He opened his email to see the agenda and was reading it when Quinn slid into the chair opposite him.

Her face was alive with a wide smile, her eyes dancing as she told him, "I received an email that my boss snagged a spot for me at a conference at Harvard on Thursday and Friday. I'm excited for two more nights in the city." She shimmied with delight.

He smiled. "My boss sent a similar message. Do you have enough clothes for two extra days? Because I do not."

She laughed. "That won't be a problem for me. You can send your clothes to the hotel laundry. They pick them up in the morning, and you'll have them back in the evening."

The server came to their table, and Sam ordered another beer while Quinn asked for a glass of white wine.

When the drinks arrived, Quinn took a swallow of her wine and exhaled deeply. "What do you want to talk about?"

How do I start? I guess I'll dive right in. Sam avoided Quinn's eyes as he began. "I moved out of my comfort zone when I started dating Norah. She's incredibly smart and accomplished. I've learned so much from her and the work she does for the state." He concentrated on his bottle of beer, obliterating its label as his fingers nervously fiddled with it. "She's an exceptional mother—"

Quinn put her hand up. Sam stopped mid-sentence, and Quinn said, "Is this what you wanted to talk to me about? Is this more of your effort to show me how you moved beyond your blue-collar roots? I'm happy for you, but it feels a little bit like you're trying to rub my nose in how great your life has turned out." She rose from her chair.

Sam scrambled to his feet and grabbed her arm. "Wait, Quinn. Please stay. That wasn't my intention. I-I..." he stuttered, unable to finish his thought. He knew his face was crumpled in pain.

Pulling back her arm, she asked, "What's going on, Sam?"

"I-I... Stay, please."

Slowly, she sat back down.

Sam took a long drink of his beer. *Just say it.* "Norah and I are splitting. That's why I was so late on Monday morning. As I was walking out the door, she told me that she had rented a house in a nearby town." At Quinn's slight gasp, he dropped his eyes. "I don't know why I started out telling you about her. It isn't my intention to make you feel bad. I'm a wreck, Quinn." He kept his eyes focused on the table until he could raise his face to look at her again.

"Wow." Quinn's hand reached across the table to rest gently on his arm. "Was this unexpected? I thought from our conversation yesterday that everything was good in your life."

"I wasn't honest with you. That's why I wanted to talk to you tonight. I know it was wrong that I was less than truthful. Especially after the accusations I hurled at the end of our relationship. It wasn't unexpected, but the timing was a surprise." He took a deep breath and finished his beer.

The server came by, and Quinn ordered another beer for him and a glass of wine for herself. She gave him time to gather his thoughts.

"Things haven't been good for a long time," he admitted. "Everything was great for a while because, you know, it's always good in the beginning. A couple of days after I found out we were going to have a baby was the first time I asked her to marry me." He rubbed one hand on the back of his neck. "You must remember how my parents hammered that into me. If you knock a girl up, you marry her."

"Your dad was adamant about that. He scared me."

Sam bobbed his head. "He scared all of us. The day Piper was born was the greatest day of my life. I can't begin to describe the joy I felt when I held her in my arms. That was the second time I asked Norah to marry me."

He looked away, taking a long pause as the sadness sank in. His gaze returned to Quinn, and he tried to smile. "I'm telling you about the proposals because you mentioned marriage last night. You're right—I always thought I'd be married, and if it was up to me, I would be. Obviously, Norah turned down both of those proposals, and eventually she told me she doesn't believe in marriage, doesn't believe a piece of paper legitimizes a relationship. We love Piper, she's the light of our lives, but after a while even that love couldn't override the things about me that drive Norah crazy."

He could see Quinn's surprise. "Like what?" she asked.

"Like I'm easily distracted, and I can be messy. I don't expect her to pick up after me. We agreed early on that I'd do the cooking, but keeping the house tidy would be her responsibility. That's important to her, and it means nothing to me." He shook his head. "She thinks I don't pull my weight in our relationship. We started not getting along—not loud noisy fights because that's not our style, but there was a lot of tension in the house. About eighteen months ago, Piper started stuttering."

He took out his phone. "Listen, this is the message from this morning."

D-D-Daddy, I c-can't wait t-till t-t-tomorrow when you're home.

"Oh, Sam."

"I know." He studied the phone, rubbing his finger on the case. "We sought all kinds of treatment, and nothing helped. We've been going to couples counseling, and they suggested a trial separation. I have a friend with a cabin on a lake, so I moved there for the summer. Piper split her time between us, which I thought would confuse her, but she thrived. The stuttering stopped after a few weeks, so we knew it was a response to the tension between Norah and me."

He drained his beer and signaled the server for another. "The funny thing was that we started getting along better and had a good summer. Two months ago, I moved back home. Things went okay for the first month, and then they fell apart. We have the same issues that we had before, and three weeks ago, Piper started stuttering again." He paused. "I knew we were going to end up splitting, but we hadn't talked about how we were going to do it. You know, which one of us would move out and how Pip would split her time."

Wait, that's not how it went. "Actually, that's not true," he said. "Norah made it clear she expected me to leave again." He shook his head and wrapped his hand around the beer bottle that had just arrived. "It's for keeps this time. I knew the summer was temporary, but there's not going to be any coming back from this move. I've put my body and soul into that house, and I won't walk away from it. Plus, I'm afraid if I leave, she'll somehow twist things to make it appear that I abandoned her and Piper."

He took a long swallow of his beer and started playing with the label again. "So we ignored the subject, which is typical with us." He raised his eyes, meeting Quinn's. "And now Norah's taken things into her own hands. Monday morning hit me exceptionally hard."

"All those things you mentioned that bother her... They didn't just start. I mean no offense, but you were messy and scattered when we were together. I'm assuming you feel like you do share the load."

He leaned back in his chair. "I think so. I have total responsibility for Pip in the morning. Which I love. I've learned to do French braids, and I can place two perfect pigtails." Sam managed to smile at Quinn. "I get her ready for school and drop her off. And believe it or not, she is generally on time. I pick her up at the end of the day, take care of any-thing she needs, and then I make dinner. We share bedtime duties. Norah's job is demanding, and she's driven, so I do what I can during the week to make our lives function."

"When the weekend comes, I want to play—take Piper hiking, go to the beach—but Norah's obsessed with getting all the things done that didn't happen during the week. And yes, I'll confess, occasionally she finds socks that I've left in the living room."

Quinn giggled. "I'm sorry, but I'm thinking of how mad my mother used to get about socks being left all over the house. Have you ever considered that you might suffer from ADHD?"

"Attention deficit..." He looked to Quinn for the rest of the words.

She completed the phrase. "Hyperactivity disorder."

"I don't consider myself hyperactive."

"It's the acronym that's used. You don't necessarily have to be frenzied or overactive."

He shrugged. "Do you remember me telling you I had special ed services in grade school? I was never told about a diagnosis, but I know my parents didn't want me medicated. Once I started high school and then college, I wasn't the best student, but I did okay without accommodations. ADHD is a learning disability, isn't it? I'm not a ten-year-old who can't concentrate."

"ADHD in adults is a thing. It hampers the ability to stay on task, which makes everyday life more difficult. There's a great deal of evidence that medicating adult ADHD results in an enhanced quality of life." She reached her hand over and put it on his. "I'm not saying it's the answer to all your problems, but it's something to think about. Do you have the same type of issues with her? Are there things that drive you crazy?"

"She's tightly wound, wants everything just so, and is compulsive about being on time. There's a lot of nagging, which, yeah, drives me nuts." He stopped and drummed his fingers on the table. "On the drive here, I was wracking my brain, trying to figure out what I could do to make it work, to get back to what we had in the beginning. Last night, I realized that it's over. I won't fight any longer. It's not good for any of us."

Sam's arms had been resting on the table, and he leaned back in his chair. "Why are you so easy to talk to? From that first day in health class, I've been able to jabber at you non-stop."

Quinn shrugged and sipped her wine.

Sam grinned. "Of course, it was all soliloquies until you finally started talking back to me. Ten years, and I've picked up right where I left off. However, you are talking a little more now."

Quinn grinned. "I'm better than I was, but I'll never be able to go on like you do."

"Is that an insult or a compliment?"

"Take it as you wish. So, this is what you wanted to talk to me about? I appreciate you being honest. I knew something was off last night when I asked why only one child."

Chapter 10
More, Now Drunken Confessions

Sam

SAM SIGHED AND GAZED at Quinn. "No, there's more." The server came by, and he ordered another beer and glass of wine for Quinn. He tried to remember how many beers he'd had.

He took a deep breath. "If Norah found out about me spending this time with you, it would piss her off."

Quinn sat back in her chair and raised her eyebrows, looking incredulous. "What? Why? We were over a long time ago, a *very* long time ago. There's nothing to fear from me."

Gazing into her eyes, Sam said, "She thinks I never recovered from you. That we have unfinished business."

Sam could see how much this admission surprised Quinn. She took a sip of her wine then finally asked, "Well, is she right?"

He thought over that question for a few seconds before starting to talk. "I don't like the way things ended. When you left for college, I started going to the bars. I swear, Quinn, I wasn't looking for anyone. I missed you so much, and I wanted to be around my friends, to be distracted. Ginger was always around, part of the gang. Things went south with you, and there she was, stroking my ego, picking up the pieces."

After a pause, he admitted, "If she hadn't been there, I would have tried to work things out with you. We had that argument, but I didn't realize when I stormed away from your house that it was truly the end for us. Ginger saw the texts you sent, trying to get me to come back, and she told me how to respond."

Sam took a swallow of his beer. "Calling you a liar? Saying you were untrustworthy? And all the rest of it? Ginger's words. I laid everything on you, and that was so wrong. I'm even more embarrassed to admit that than I was to tell you about Norah leaving."

Tears came into Quinn's eyes, and he watched as she blinked furiously, trying unsuccessfully to prevent them from spilling down her face.

Reaching across the table, Sam wiped a tear from her cheek. Quinn opened her mouth, but no sound came out.

She took a deep breath and tried again. "Julie told me you were seeing someone. I wasn't sure whether to believe her or not. It's hard to hear that it was true. She told you what to text me? Really? You couldn't come up with the words on your own?"

"I allowed myself to be manipulated in so many ways throughout that relationship. She wanted to be sure what I said would leave no doubt. She was afraid that you'd be able to talk me into staying with you. I'm ashamed, I'd never use that kind of language with you."

"Oh, you left no doubt. I was crushed. And I knew what you were saying wasn't your words."

"I was such a prick. I'm so sorry, Quinn. This has eaten me up for years. When I finally ended it with Ginger, I was already friends with Norah and had thought about asking her out. But..." He stopped. Quinn's expression had changed from tearful to something Sam couldn't read. "I'm sorry. I know this is difficult for you to hear."

"It is, but I'm okay."

"I still wondered if there was any chance for us, but I didn't know how to approach you. I saw you in the park, so I stopped. You were there with Julie, and as I walked toward the two of you, you went to your car. I talked to Julie for a long time until it was too awkward to continue waiting."

Tears returned to her eyes. Sam held her in his gaze as Quinn finished her glass of wine. Finally, blinking away the tears, she snorted. "You realize Julie is the common denominator. She's the one who told you I had sex with someone in Virginia, isn't she?"

Sam nodded.

"I knew it had to be her. She's the only one I told. And then she told me about you and Ginger. Plus, that day in the park, she had told me she'd heard you were breaking up with Ginger. It's rich when you think about how she treated Casey. She cheated on him the entire time they were together. Did you know that?"

"I did. I never told Casey. It wasn't my story to tell. But I was happy when they finally split."

"Me too. I haven't talked to her since that day in the park."

"Did she tell you what we talked about?"

Quinn shook her head. "Not really. I asked, and she said you confirmed that you had left Ginger and that you were interested in someone at your office, but that was it."

"I asked if you were seeing anyone. I told her I wanted to apologize to you and wanted to talk to you before going forward with Norah. I gave her my phone number to give you."

Quinn leaned back in stunned silence. "Julie didn't tell me any of that."

The server had placed another beer and glass of wine on their table. Sam hadn't noticed when Quinn signaled for them. "Would you have called?"

"I don't know." After a second, Quinn snickered. "You know what I would have done? I would have talked to my mother, and she would have urged me to call, so I would have. My mom was always Team Sam."

Sam smiled faintly. "I loved your mom." He picked up his new beer and studied it. "When I didn't hear from you, I went ahead with Norah. I don't regret that. It's given me Piper, and she's the greatest thing in my life." He laughed a little. "I love being a dad. When she curls up in my lap and whispers 'I love you' in my ear, I feel like my heart's going to explode. That's what sucks about Norah moving out. I'll get over her—the relationship's been falling apart for years—but not seeing Pip every day is going to hurt." He took a swallow of the beer. "Still, I've never stopped wondering what it would be like if you and I had stayed together."

"I'm not trying to blame things on Julie. I know I was wrong to have sex with someone else and to lie to you about it. That's all on me."

"What made me the angriest was that I wasn't enough for you." Seeing the question in Quinn's eyes, Sam continued, "You were all I wanted. When I went away to college, I never even glanced at another woman. I lived for the weekends I came home to you. Before you left, we had plans to see each other once a month. Then the first month wasn't even over, but you wanted to find out what other guys had to offer. That hurt. I thought we'd be together forever."

He blinked back his own tears. "I realize how stupid that sounds. You were fifteen when we met, sixteen when we started dating. How many people stay in their first relationship forever? So stupid." His arms were folded on the table, and he lowered his head onto them.

After several seconds, Quinn reached across the table, placing her hand on one of his arms and shaking it. "Sam, are you okay? Sam."

He raised his head and reached for his now empty beer bottle. "Did you wonder what it would have been like, a life with me?"

"I tried not to. I shoved your memory into a vault, and I thought I'd thrown away the key."

Sam chuckled. "That's me. The key to unlocking your heart. Jesse told me I had to tell you all that. Said I'd feel better. Well, maybe not all of it."

"Do you?"

"Do I what?"

"Feel better?"

He thought about that. "I don't know. And I'm not sure if it's getting all this out in the open or the beer that's driving how I feel right now. This is much more beer than I usually drink." Glancing around the bar, he realized there was only one other table with people still sitting at it. "Damn, it's late."

The server came over, and Sam asked for the check. He pulled out his wallet and as he searched for his credit card, he said, "Can we make the trip to Harvard together on Thursday? I'm intimidated about going there." When Quinn laughed, he asked, "What? What's so funny?"

She blinked and said, "That was kind of an abrupt change of subject, but yes, I'm intimidated as well, and traveling together would be good."

"This won't make things weird between us, will it? Because I don't want things to be weird. I had to get it out, and we never have to talk about it again. I don't want you to think that I've spent ten years pining for you because I haven't." He paused. "Oh man, that sounds mean. I'm not trying to be mean. I've wondered what life with you would be like, but mostly I've liked my life with Norah and Piper. Been happy, mostly happy. Well, at the beginning I was happy. Being a dad makes me happy. I'm babbling, aren't I?"

Relief that everything was out in the open, coursed through his body. *Or it's the alcohol.*

They stood, pushing their chairs back, and Sam staggered before regaining his footing.

"Sam, I'm going to walk with you to your room, to make sure you get there. Is that okay?" Quinn asked.

"Sure. You think you're more sober than I am? I saw quite a few wine glasses on that table." He wobbled again, and Quinn put her hand on his arm to steady him.

The elevator stopped on the seventh floor, and they walked to his room. The door didn't open with his first or second insertion of the key.

Quinn checked the door number. "Are you sure we're at the right room?"

Sam nodded and tried the key once more. The lock clicked, and the door swung open. Turning, he started to tell her no more babysitting was necessary.

Instead, he reached out for her. His arms enveloped her, and she stepped into them. His plan was to give her a quick hug like the day before, but it quickly grew into more as they came together. His grasp tightened, and he felt her relaxing into the hug, wrapping her arms around his neck, reaching her hands up to his hair.

No other woman had ever fit against him like Quinn did. Her breasts crushed against his chest, arousing him, and he knew she could feel it too. His hands moved along her back, traveling down to gently stroke the curve of her butt. Her fingers ran through his hair, reminding him of all the other hugs they had shared.

He pulled back. "All this time, I've missed you so much. You were my best friend." He studied her face and then leaned in, wanting to taste her lips, before stopping himself.

No, this is a mistake. Reluctantly Sam pushed her away. "You should go." Backing into his room, he shut the door, flopped on the bed, and passed out.

Sam groaned and rolled over in bed, reaching for Quinn and coming up empty-handed. *What the fuck?*

He opened his eyes, squinting at the overhead light that he'd forgotten to turn off, surprised to find himself still fully dressed, lying in the middle of the bed with his head pounding. The previous night came rushing back to him. He'd told Quinn about Norah leaving, and more importantly, he'd told her the genesis of all the accusations he'd hit her with at the end of their relationship. And he remembered drinking beer, a lot of beer.

I must have passed out as soon as I walked in here. I was dreaming about that first fight Quinn and I had. The one where when it was over, we lay on the lawn gazing at the stars and expressing our love for each other.

He climbed off the bed and stumbled to the bathroom. *Oh my God, standing is worse than lying down.* He needed some ibuprofen but knew he didn't have any.

Walking back to the bedroom, he undressed, turned off the lights, and crawled under the covers. Before falling back to sleep, he remembered hugging Quinn after she walked him to his room. Really, really hugging her. He'd wanted more, wanted to draw her into the room to explore every part of her body. And she... She didn't hesitate or hold back. She leaned in, deeper and tighter.

Yet, somehow, he'd pushed her away to go into his room alone, where he passed out to dream of the boy and girl they had been.

Chapter 11
Kryptonite

Quinn

QUINN MADE HER WAY to the twenty-fifth floor with her insides blazing. *Was he about to pull me into his room for more than a hug? Would I have gone?*

The Quinn of a few years ago would have, but she'd become more discerning. Having sex with Sam Carpenter right now would be a big mistake—he was hurting and searching for something to ease the pain. She'd had plenty of one-night stands, and they'd done nothing to fill the emptiness or end the sadness. And they'd both had too much to drink. So, no, if Sam hadn't broken it off, then she would have.

But, oh, that hug.

Trying to counteract all that wine, she washed her face, drank two bottles of water, and took ibuprofen before taking a moment to stand in front of the windows. But the city lights did nothing to calm the turmoil Sam's confession had caused in her.

Most of what he said was totally unexpected. It had always been a mystery to her how he'd walked away from all they meant to each other back then. And now she knew it hadn't been easy for him to do that. *He thought about coming back to me. Of course. I was so stupid.*

That day in the park was etched into her psyche. It had come to mind while she was telling Angie about how Sam always had someone ready to move on with. He'd mentioned her hiding in the car, and he was right—but it wasn't only to avoid seeing him. She hid because she was afraid. Two years after their breakup, nightmares about the angry words he'd used were still plaguing her.

I don't know whether to be angry or sad. They'd both made mistakes, and anger had consumed her for years after the breakup. Anger at herself because she'd had sex with someone else and she'd lied to Sam about it, and anger at him for not forgiving her.

I can't go back to that anger. I'm sad that our missteps ruined the relationship. And Julie, one of my closest friends... How does she live with herself?

Quinn's thoughts went back to that hug, arousing her more than she had been in a long time. *Dammit, he still turns me on even after all these years. Or maybe it's that I haven't had anyone touch me in such a long time.*

Quinn stepped back from the window and stripped off her clothes. She climbed into bed and reached down to touch herself. The climax would come quickly tonight, fueled by memories of Sam and their embrace. His erection had been evident through their clothes, and she imagined having him inside her. Her breasts had been crushed against his chest, making her remember what it was like to have his mouth on them.

Her hand moved faster, and she grew wetter and wetter. On a final stroke, she came with a moan, wave after wave of climax sweeping over her.

When the orgasm ended, she turned onto her side, sated, and promptly fell asleep.

Quinn did not wake up at her usual early hour. It was tough to force her eyes open at seven o'clock. She wanted to sleep longer but knew coffee and food would make her feel better.

She pulled a red sweater over her head, hoping a pop of color might help her look better than she felt. The concealer she dabbed on the circles under her eyes was only marginally successful, and while working on her face, she wondered how Sam was feeling.

He's needy. I wish I hadn't told him we could go to Harvard together tomorrow. I know what happens to me around needy men.

She felt wobbly and sat on the bed, trying to pull herself together before heading to the breakfast buffet. *Thank God I stuck to wine, otherwise I'm sure I would have been barfing all night long. I'm such a lightweight.*

The hug popped into her mind. She remembered how hot it had made her and thought about how it was making her feel right now. The uneasy feeling in her stomach wasn't entirely from the wine. *What the hell am I doing? I do not want to get involved with Sam Carpenter again. I don't want to be involved with any man. And even though he said it's over with Norah, he's not available. Get yourself together, Quinn.*

In the line for the buffet, Angie pounced on her, asking, "How were the drinks?"

"We closed the bar, and I drank way too much wine. Don't talk so loudly." Quinn smiled and motioned with her hands for Angie to keep her voice soft.

She could see the surprise on Angie's face. "You usually make sure I drink the bulk of the wine! What did Sam want to talk about?"

Quinn wondered where to start. Angie was going to jump all over the news that Sam was apparently no longer with Norah. Her romantic brain would read more into it than there was.

But it was inevitable. "Well, he started out by telling me how great Norah is—that's his, God, what do you call her? Girl-friend, life partner, baby mama? Whatever she is, her name is Norah, and evidently, she's amazing." Quinn's words dripped with sarcasm. "After a few minutes of that, I stopped him and thought about leaving, because I didn't need to hear what a wonderful creature he ended up with."

"Whoa. You go, girl! Tell him how it is."

"Yeah. He grabbed my arm and asked me to stay, saying that wasn't his intention. His eyes were filled with tears, so I sat back down. Then he told me that Norah is leaving him and the reason he was so late on Monday was that she dropped it on him as he was getting ready to leave for the conference."

"That's low."

Quinn gave her a condensed version of what Sam had shared, ending by saying, "He was emotional even just telling me about it, so get any romantic notions out of your head. He's not thinking about starting something up with me." *There, I've nipped that discussion right in the bud.*

"What caused the tension between them? I always like to hear what makes relationships unravel."

"He's messy."

"Messy? They've been together several years and have a daughter, and she's going to blow up their home because he's messy? That's messed up." Angie's voice went up an octave in righteous indignation. "You see what I did there, right?"

"That's truly one thing he mentioned. But there's some other stuff, like he's scattered, doesn't do enough—you know, the typical reasons. And.... apparently, Norah has some issues with me."

"Ah, now that's the stuff I want to hear. What issues? Did he go right to her from you? Was she his exit strategy?"

Quinn smiled at how Angie had picked up her phrase. "No, not at all. There was another woman and two years in between. Still, Norah thinks he and I have unfinished business."

"And…" Angie prompted.

"And apparently she's right, because he apologized for the way things ended between us." She described how Sam told her Ginger had scripted the nasty text messages he had sent her after they argued. "I always felt like it wasn't him talking to me, that they weren't his words, and it turns out I was right."

"Wow. It took all evening to get all of that out?"

"All evening and copious amounts of beer and wine. I walked him to his room because I wasn't sure he'd be able to get there on his own." Quinn felt herself blushing.

Angie pounced on it. "What are you leaving out? An apology for crappy behavior would not embarrass you like that."

"He hugged me. A hug to end all hugs. I had a strong reaction to it."

Angie raised her eyebrows inquisitively.

"Yeah, that way. It made me all hot and bothered."

"Yes!" Angie squealed and raised her fist in the air.

Quinn put her hands over her ears. "My head! Please!"

Angie grinned. "Sorry. But no pulling you into his room for a passion-filled reunion?"

Quinn frowned. "No. I thought he was going to, and I wasn't sure how I was going to react to that. I think I would have backed away, but I'm not sure. I was into it." She sighed. "When we were first dating, my mom hammered into me—and him, as well—that you don't make stupid decisions because passion sweeps you away. That having sex was much better as the result of a well-thought-out decision, and it was, when we did it for the first time." Quinn drained her coffee cup and rose to leave. "I didn't always heed her advice, but it stayed with me. Maybe it stayed with him, too, because he left me at the door."

They started walking toward the conference room with Angie advising Quinn to latch onto what could turn out to be an epic love story.

As they were passing the elevator, the doors opened, and Sam walked out in front of them. He paused when he saw them, and Quinn asked him how he was.

"Hungover. Extremely hungover." He smiled a little. "How about you?"

"I'm a little shaky."

His glance settled on Angie. "You must be Angie. I'm Sam. Quinn and I knew each other in high school. See, Quinn?" He playfully bumped against her shoulder. "Your manners are as bad as mine, not introducing me to your friend."

Quinn rolled her eyes.

"She gave me way too much beer last night," he told Angie. "Hey, do you have any ibuprofen with you?"

Quinn dug into her bag to find some.

He popped them into his mouth and swallowed hard. "You women carry everything, Band-Aids, ibuprofen, lollipops, bubbles. Prepared for anything." They reached his conference room, and he started to enter and then turned back. "If they don't have coffee and water like they did the last two mornings, I'm going to cry."

When Sam was out of earshot, Angie hit Quinn on the arm. "He's funny! Lollipops? Bubbles? What do you think that's about? And he's cute!"

Quinn smiled. "Did you think fifteen-year-old me was going to chase after a boy who wasn't cute?"

As they sat down, Angie asked her if she had already checked out. Quinn told her about the text message, letting her know about the conference at Harvard and the extra nights in the hotel.

Angie sighed. "Two more nights in a hotel would be heavenly, but my house would be a wreck if I were away for the entire week."

Later, as they were walking out of the session, Angie asked quietly, "He's your kryptonite, isn't he? A guy in need of rescue."

Quinn hadn't shared many details about her dating life with Angie, but she had talked about her attraction to needy men. She nodded ruefully. "He is, and I'm trying to avoid that. I want someone who can be an equal partner, not someone I have to prop up."

They arrived in the lobby, where Angie picked up her luggage. "I'll see you at our weekend in January."

"You bet. And we'll be in touch during the next few weeks while we finish our papers." Quinn ran her hand through her hair. "Sam's stay was extended too. He's going to the conference at Harvard. He already asked me if we can travel there together."

Angie's eyes widened. "All right!" She reached out to fist-bump Quinn and was left hanging. Angie frowned and lowered her fist. "You need to get after that. It could be a fun fling. You don't have to make a lifelong commitment. Have a little fun."

She grinned and pulled Quinn into a goodbye hug.

Quinn returned the hug then shook her head. "I don't think that's a good idea."

Chapter 12
Norah Calls

Sam

THE IBUPROFEN QUINN GAVE Sam hadn't done enough. His head was still pounding when his session finished, and his stomach wasn't feeling great either.

Walking toward the lobby, he debated how to spend his afternoon. He saw two wing chairs in front of a fireplace and sat for a minute to gather his thoughts. After a few minutes, his phone pinged with a message from Norah, and his heart sank, wondering what bad news he was going to see.

> Norah: I'd like to take Piper to my parents for Thanksgiving. We'd leave after school on Tuesday and return on Sunday. My whole family is going to be there, and we haven't seen them since the summer. I know it's a few weeks away, but my mom wants to make plans.

Her family. That meant Connecticut, a four-hour drive and almost a whole week without seeing Piper. The upcoming holiday hadn't crossed his mind.

Is this what the future is going to be? Not getting to see Pip on the holidays? Missing her excitement on Christmas morning? He sighed and rested his head on the back of the chair for a minute.

The next thing Sam knew, a family walked by with two small children who were arguing loudly, making him sit up in the chair. He caught sight of Quinn sitting in the chair next to him. Chagrined, he asked, "I was asleep, wasn't I?"

She nodded, laughing at him a bit.

Surprisingly, he felt slightly better. "What are you going to do this afternoon?"

"It's a nice day. I'm thinking of walking down to Quincy Market. There are shops and a bunch of different food stands. Being out in the fresh air will feel good. You're welcome to join me."

"I'd like that." He turned in the chair, so he was fully facing her. "Hey, Quinn, about last night. I never thought about the fact that unburdening myself might cause you pain. It was never my intention to hurt you by bringing up ancient history. I'm sorry if it did."

She gazed at him. "It hurt a little, but mostly it answered some questions I'd always had. I'm sad for how things ended between us."

Sam stood and extended his hand to pull her up with him. He brought his body to Quinn's in a quick, friendly hug and kissed the top of her head before letting go.

Half an hour later, they walked through the lobby, where the pretty, green-eyed concierge smiled and waved at Sam.

He waved back, and Quinn asked, "You're friends with the concierge?"

"Oh yeah, we go way back... all the way to Monday. I think she likes me." He winked at Quinn. "Are you jealous?"

"Why would I be?" As they stepped outside, she told him, "I'm planning to stop at one or two historical spots on the way."

"Oh no. Are you trying to educate me? You know history was never my strong suit." He glared at her in mock anger before breaking into a smile. "Hey, you're my tour guide. I have no idea about anything here."

They crossed over to Newbury Street, which was dotted with shops and small cafes, many with outdoor seating.

"This is one of the most exclusive shopping areas in the city," Quinn said. "The prices are all out of my range, but I like to window-shop and people-watch."

At the entrance to the Granary Burial Ground, she turned, leading Sam in. "Paul Revere's grave is here, as well as other historical figures' from the time of the Revolutionary War. I think it's cool to see these headstones that have been here for over two hundred years."

After touring the cemetery, they walked down Tremont Street again. Sam couldn't get over the architecture and age of the buildings. He looked over at Quinn. "This is a lot more fun and less stressful than my drive here was. After Monday morning, I swore I would never come to Boston again. But I can see what you like about the city. It's a completely different world than back home."

"Yes, exactly. I like everything about it. The buildings, the people, the history, the charge in the atmosphere. But you're right about the driving—it totally sucks. If I lived here, I wouldn't even want a car. I'd take public transportation or walk." They continued in silence for several blocks until they were at the waterfront. "Here we are. Do you want to get food now?"

He grimaced. "Not sure how food is going to sit, but it's worth a try."

They selected a cafe that had open seating, and as they were studying the menu, Sam's phone rang. He pulled it out and said, "Oh, damn, it's Norah."

"Go ahead," Quinn said. "Take the call."

Sam stood and walked to a quiet spot before answering. "Hey, sorry for not responding before. I hadn't thought about the holiday. It's fine, but I'll be home Friday night, so I want Piper from Saturday morning until Wednesday."

Norah's voice was still icy. "I'll bring her over on Saturday morning, and then you can bring her back to me at bedtime."

"Are you crazy? I'm not doing that! I want her all night. I want to put her to bed and have her wake me up in the morning."

"Sam, I took the furniture when I left. There isn't anywhere for Pip to sleep."

His face contorted as the anger built inside him. "Did you take all of it?"

"All the stuff that I brought in." Piper's bed had been Norah's when she was a child.

Dammit! How can she do this to me? "I've been away all week. I miss her." He missed Piper so much. "I want her from Saturday to Wednesday. I'll figure something out for sleeping arrangements."

Norah was silent for a second before responding. "What if you have her tomorrow and Sunday then bring her back to me Sunday night so she can go to school from here on Monday morning? I want her to get adjusted to the new place."

Sam worked to keep his emotions under control. *I can't believe this. She's trying to shut me out of Pip's life.* He took a deep breath and tried to maintain a civil tone. "No, it's nonnegotiable. I want her at the house Saturday morning, and she'll stay with me until Wednesday."

Norah sighed. "Fine. What time?"

"Nine o'clock. I'll see you then."

He shoved the phone back into his pocket and gazed into the distance, gathering himself again, before walking back to the table where Quinn was waiting.

"I'm not hungry," he said, trying to lighten his voice and failing miserably. "I'm going back to the hotel. You don't have to come with me."

"What's going on?"

"I can't talk right now. I don't mean to be rude." He raised a hand to emphasize his point. "I just can't."

Quinn remained seated. "I'm going to stay here. I want to do some shopping."

Sam muttered "whatever" before he turned to start the walk back.

He retraced their steps, minus the detour to the Burial Ground. It wasn't the light, fun stroll they'd had on the way down. He walked fast, staring straight ahead, not seeing any of the landmarks Quinn had pointed out earlier.

Once back in his room, he kicked off his shoes and dug running clothes out of his bag. *My head is still killing me, but I have to do something to work off this anger.*

Sam started out on the same route as Monday and Tuesday but at a faster pace. For the first five miles, he concentrated only on the movement, his footfalls, and his breathing. It took thirty-five minutes, a seven-minute-per-mile pace, only slightly slower than it would be in a race.

Not ready to turn back, he pounded all the way down to the waterfront. He paused there to get his bearings, hands on his knees, trying to catch his breath. He watched the boats in the harbor as he thought about the conversation with Norah.

She took the damn furniture! Oh, not everything, only the stuff that *she* brought into the house. Which was nearly everything. Most importantly, she had taken Piper's bed. Her idea that he would only have Pip during the day was insane. Putting Piper to bed after reading a story with her was one of his favorite parts of the day. If Norah thought Piper wasn't going to be with him half the time, she was delusional.

He took off again, his turbulent emotions keeping his return pace the same as it had been on the run out.

Arriving back at the hotel, Sam leaned against the wall to catch his breath. Quinn popped into his head. Damn, he'd been crappy to her, hadn't told her what was going on as he went into a dark, angry place. *I acted like my father. I need to apologize.*

Quinn

Quinn spent a couple of hours walking around Quincy Market, happy to have some time to herself. She'd been with either Angie or Sam during nearly every free moment, and that wasn't what she had planned. She bought Christmas presents for her friends and family and found some decor items for her townhouse.

Quinn enjoyed the walk back to the hotel and stood at the window when she reached her room. She hadn't been able to hear the conversation between Sam and Norah, but she had watched as his anger became apparent through his body language.

Ever since he sat down next to me, we've been playing this little get-reacquainted game, complete with true confessions and a hug that rocked me to my core. I've distracted him from thinking about what's waiting for him at home. Damn, damn, damn.

This was exactly what she tried to explain to Angie about being an exit strategy. If someone else was there to buffer the pain, then it never got dealt with. Hence the "unfinished business" that Norah suspected there was between them. Sam needed to work this shit out with Norah.

Quinn went to the pool, knowing that a swim would wash away the rest of her hangover.

Should I text Sam to let him know where I am?

No. Angie was right. The vulnerability—Sam's pain—was her kryptonite, and she needed to stay away from it.

Chapter 13
Harvard Yard

Sam

SAM STOPPED AT HIS room to change. *She's probably in the pool.* Even if Quinn wasn't there, the pool and then the hot tub would feel good.

The pool was empty, which meant he'd have to text Quinn. He jumped in and swam a few laps before flipping onto his back to gaze up at the sky through the glass ceiling and wonder what it would look like in a snowstorm. Or on a clear night with stars twinkling.

Between the run and the laps in the pool, his hangover was fading. A few minutes relaxing in the warm bubbles of the hot tub would finish it off, he hoped. As he approached the alcove with the hot tub, he saw Quinn soaking in it.

He approached cautiously and stood at the edge. "I was an asshole earlier. I'm sorry. I shouldn't have left you like that with no explanation."

Quinn stared up at him for what seemed like forever without responding. Sam wondered if she was going to light into him for being so rude, but instead she finally said, "I could be angry, but I actually enjoyed having time on my own." When Sam sighed with relief, she tilted her head at him. "Are you going to get in?"

He sank into the bubbles and apologized again. "I'm so sorry for earlier. I needed some time to process what Norah told me. I hadn't thought about the logistics of her moving out, what she'd be taking with her. And it turns out what she took was most of our furniture. I also hadn't thought about how she was accomplishing this move. She must've gotten a truck and arranged for help, so she's been planning this for a while." He rubbed his hand along his jaw. "She didn't wake up on Monday morning and decide that she was going to leave me. Obviously, I knew she had found a place, but it didn't occur to me she had all these pieces together, making it so she could leave in the three days I would be gone. While I was living my everyday life, she was plotting this move." His voice cracked a little on the word *plotting*. "How could I have been so oblivious?"

Quinn didn't respond but seemed to be listening, so he continued. "I need to figure out what I'm doing in the future. I can't keep going merrily along, letting life happen to me. The furniture is a perfect example. I'm thirty-one years old, and all I own is a couch, and a television. I moved in with Ginger, then I moved in with Norah, so I have nothing." He felt like such an idiot.

They sat in silence amid the soothing jets and the warmth of the water.

Finally, Sam sighed. "I need to figure out what Piper is going to sleep on. And then I need to make a plan for how I'm going to live in a house with no furniture."

"Will you stay there?"

"We split the mortgage. I don't know. My salary is good, but Norah's is better, so she pays more." He scoffed. "Our relationship is closer to a business partnership than a loving union of two people. All the bills are split proportionally. Which I guess works, but it lacks the warmth I envisioned for my life."

Quinn nodded but remained quiet.

"So I don't know if I'll stay there," he said. "I want to, but there's a lot to figure out. That's why I don't want to rush out and buy furniture. I've been trying to figure out what she left." He shook his head and sank down farther into the water. "It's the only home Piper has ever known. I don't want to leave that." He closed his eyes and leaned his head back.

Quinn remained quiet.

Finally, his eyes opened. "I'm sorry. I don't mean to lay all this on you."

Quinn shook her head. "I don't know what to say, Sam. You've got a lot going on."

Sam forced a smile. "That's putting it mildly. Did you eat earlier? Because I'm starving, and I feel like I owe you food."

"I had a cup of clam chowder, but I could eat something."

"We passed a pizza place on Monday before we took that bridge across the road. Do you want to go there?"

Quinn nodded. "Their food is delicious. I know it's early, but let's go now. Maybe we'll be ahead of the dinner crowd. Meet in the lobby?"

"Absolutely."

Getting to the restaurant early was perfect, as they were led to a table right away. The server came to take their order, asking about drinks first. They grinned at each other, then they both ordered sodas along with a pizza to share.

As the server walked away, Sam said, "I may never drink alcohol again."

"I know what you mean. I never saw you drink like that." She laughed. "And for that matter, you never saw me drink either."

Sam took a moment before answering. "I avoided it for a long time, but I've had a few drunken binges over the years since I last saw you. I don't want to be like my dad. I watched him get drunk far too often and saw the black moods that resulted from it. I kind of went into one of those after that conversation with Norah earlier." He paused. "Again, I'm sorry. I never want to be like my father."

"Is that still an issue for him?"

"Honestly? I have no idea. I don't see much of my parents. They've only seen Piper a handful of times."

"What about Joe and Matt?" she asked, referring to his brothers.

He shook his head. "Don't see them either. We all went our separate ways." He laughed a little bitterly, realizing something. "Joe lives here in Boston. It never occurred to me to get in touch with him." *I can't believe I never even thought about Joe. Way to be self-absorbed, Sam.*

"That's kind of sad. You three were so close."

"I know." *When did that happen?* "When Norah and I moved in together, she became my family. And Jesse is like a brother to me, so I'm close to his family. Joe sent me a few texts over the summer asking me to go north with him. He and his wife split earlier this year, and he's been going up to my parents', working on some project he wants me to see. I can't do it. I have no desire to spend time with my father." He took a drink of his soda and as he put the glass down, said, "I'm shocked that Joe does. Dad was as rough on him as he was on me." He shook his head. "It is what it is. I bet you're still close with your parents."

"I am. We're very close."

"They were so awesome. I was more comfortable at your house than I ever was at my own."

Their pizza arrived, and as they each took a slice, Sam said, "I was thinking while I changed. I'll buy a couple of those inflatable mattresses for Piper and me until I figure out the furniture."

"You'll need sheets, blankets, and pillows." Quinn bit into her pizza.

Sam groaned, putting down his slice and pulling out his phone. "You're right. I need to make a list, so I don't forget something."

As he was tapping on his phone, Quinn said, "If you have an extra bedroom, you could try renting it out. There are always people at the hospital searching for housing like that."

"That's an idea." He considered how that could work. "Both of our names are on the deed, so that's something that needs to be disentangled, and how we are going to divide Piper's time between us. I need a lawyer."

They talked for two hours. Sam had extensive notes for steps to take, and he felt more in control than he had since Monday morning.

Quinn

They were still at the restaurant when Quinn checked her watch and realized it was only six o'clock. "This may sound crazy," she said, "but I'd like to go over to the Harvard campus. I've never been to Cambridge, and I get anxious about going somewhere unfamiliar to me. I'd like to get that out of the way tonight, kind of get the lay of the land. Do you want to go with me?"

"I never would have thought of visiting the campus, but it's a great idea. Anything to prevent tomorrow morning from being like Monday."

Quinn ordered a rideshare, and they were at the campus in twenty minutes. She asked the driver how long it would take in the morning and was told the trip would be twice as long.

Sam grimaced, shaking his head. "I don't know how people live with this traffic every day."

As she was deciding which direction they should walk, she noticed him gazing at her. "What? Do I have food on my face or something?"

"No, I'm surprised at how much you've changed. How confident you are."

"I had to learn a lot of things after I left Vermont. I hated how timid and insecure I was in high school. You must remember that. My biggest goal in life was to banish that child forever. It's one reason I went so far away for college. I had to rely on myself there, and I've mostly succeeded."

They walked around in companionable silence, looking at the historic buildings and people-watching.

After a few minutes, Sam said, "I admire how adventurous you are. I've gone the other direction. My life has been sedate and predictable. Work and home, that's about it. And home's not that different from where we grew up."

"Having a child counts as a major adventure."

"I suppose. But it wasn't planned, at least not on my part. Don't get me wrong—I was thrilled when Norah told me she was pregnant. A little overwhelmed at first but thrilled that we were going to bring a child into the world. There's no feeling like hearing that news, except for maybe when the baby is born." He bumped against her shoulder. "I hope you get to experience that someday."

"Me too. I'll confess, I have my moments when the old insecurities rear their head. Like Monday morning. I deliberately sat where I was, hoping no one would sit next to me. I was pissed when I heard the door open because I knew whoever was coming in would want that seat."

Sam laughed. "Sorry about that."

She shrugged and said with a smile, "It wasn't as bad as it could have been. Hey, I think this is our building." She could see where they would be dropped off in the morning but wasn't sure which entrance they'd be using.

They continued exploring the campus. After a while, Sam asked, "Do you remember the movie your mom suggested we watch about a guy and girl on the Harvard campus? This makes me think of that."

"Oh God yes, *Love Story*. It was a big hit when she was in junior high. So sappy." Quinn shook her head and quoted the iconic line. "'Love means never having to say you're sorry.' I've found it means saying you're sorry all the time."

Sam cocked his head, and she could see the questions in his eyes. "Sorry. Geesh! See what I mean?" She laughed and turned her head away from him. "I'm letting my unpleasant experiences surface. I try not to do that."

"Anything you want to talk about?"

"Nope." Their easy conversation evaporated. The temperature had dropped at some point, and Quinn started shivering. "I'm cold. We should head back."

Once they were back at the hotel, Quinn spent a few minutes gazing out the window, as had become her routine. Sam hadn't hugged her when they reached his floor, but this hadn't been a hugging kind of night.

Now that the awkwardness between them was mostly gone, she had to acknowledge the big hole his absence had left in her life. Spending time with him now felt as natural as it had when they first met, and it scared her. Sam was not available, and she was serious about not wanting another needy guy, not even her first love.

Truthfully, do I want any man? It's been two years. Am I ready to jump back into the dating rat race?

Quinn sat on the bed and began to undress. The movie he mentioned came to mind. *Does he remember how many times I said I was sorry at the end? I begged him over and over again to forgive me. God, I was practically on my knees.*

Her two serious relationships after Sam had been with guys in dead-end jobs, barely supporting themselves and living in crappy apartments. *I did so much for them.* She gazed at the floor. *And yet every time something went wrong, I was the one apologizing.*

She stood up. *Okay, that's enough wallowing. I've moved beyond that. I'm not that girl anymore.*

Quinn's time in the city was almost over. When she was planning her trip, one thing she had intended to do was to go to her favorite restaurant in the North End. She thought about inviting Sam to go with her. She had no qualms about eating in a restaurant on her own, but she'd enjoyed the time they had spent together, and she knew he'd like the restaurant. But fear that he'd think the invitation was more than she meant it to be made her hesitate.

No. We're friends—we've gotten back to that spot. He's not thinking about moving on. He said things have been bad between him and Norah for a long time, but I still wonder if they'll try to work things out. I'll never see him again after Friday.

Exhausted from the short nights and long days filled with emotion, Quinn crawled into bed. She sent Sam a text before falling asleep.

> *Quinn: You've fed me all week. I'm taking you to dinner tomorrow night.*

Chapter 14
The Man from the Bar Buys Quinn a Chai

Quinn

QUINN WALKED INTO THE lobby at seven fifteen, but Sam was not there, even though they had agreed that they would leave the hotel at seven thirty. If he wasn't there when the rideshare arrived, she was going to leave without him. Her text from the night before still sat unanswered, and she sent another one asking where he was as her toe tapped nervous-ly.

She was glad they had gone to the Harvard campus the night before. At least she had a bit of familiarity with it now. She smiled, thinking about their walk around the campus, searching for the right building. It had been intimidating, but being with Sam eased her tension.

Sam burst through the door of the hotel as their ride pulled up.

She grimaced at him. "I didn't think you were going to make it."

"I know, I know. I didn't hear the alarm I set."

Almost as soon as the car pulled away from the hotel, they were locked up in traffic. They sat in silence until Quinn finally asked, "Are you okay? Did you get my text about dinner?"

"I did. Dinner sounds good. I had weird dreams that kept waking me up. They finally stopped, then I fell so soundly asleep I missed the alarm. Sorry."

Quinn recognized the troubled look on his face and put her hand gently on top of his. "Do you want to talk about them?"

"No. Thanks for asking, but all I can remember are bits and pieces that won't make any sense." His face relaxed a little, and he snorted. "Again, with the traffic. It's unreal."

They arrived an hour early and found the registration table. Once registered, Quinn's anxiety began to lessen. There were a variety of food kiosks throughout the lobby, and she needed something warm to drink. Sam had stayed quiet during the ride, and after comparing their materials, they realized their lecture halls were in different directions and on different floors of the building. They agreed to meet in the lobby for lunch, and Sam left.

Quinn stepped into the lengthy line at a coffee bar, happy to have time to wait. When her turn came, she ordered a chai. After the barista handed it to her, she stepped away from the kiosk and stopped to organize herself. She put her tote bag over her shoulder and switched the chai from her left hand to her right.

A student came out of nowhere at a dead run, clipping Quinn's arm as he dashed past, and her chai crashed to the floor. Other than muttering, "Sorry, sorry," he didn't break stride.

Quinn stared at the mess as a custodian hurried over with a mop and told her he would take care of it. The line for coffee had grown to fifteen or more people, and after deciding there wasn't time to wait again, she headed toward her lecture hall, disappointed at missing out on her drink.

Quinn found a seat in the middle of the room and was scrolling on her phone when a voice behind her said, "I bought you a replacement."

She whipped her head around and found herself staring into a pair of deep blue eyes.

Oh my God, it's the guy from the bar! With a sense of disbelief, she asked, "You what?" She took in his curly black hair and warm smile while waiting for him to reply.

"I was behind you in the coffee line and saw what happened. Noticed that your lanyard matched mine, so I knew we'd be in the same place. Please take it—I don't drink chai."

Quinn slowly reached for the drink, and the man gestured toward the seat next to her, asking, "Is it okay if I sit here?" He waited patiently until she nodded. "I'm Caden. Brady, like the quarterback." He winked. "No relation."

Quinn recognized the reference. When Tom Brady left the New England Patriots for another team, she'd been heartbroken. "You mean the deserter?"

"Well, there is that, but the Pats seem to have finally gotten themselves back together, so this season is going okay."

"I'd say better than okay. Undefeated for the first eight games." She grinned.

"It's not every day that I meet a beautiful woman who's a Patriots fan. I mean, you know their record, so you must be a Patriots fan. Because if you cheer for the Dolphins, I'll have to move to another seat."

Quinn laughed. "The Dolphins? Ew. No, they're the worst. Relax. I root for New England all the way. I'm Quinn Michaels, by the way. And thanks for the drink. I can't believe how rude that kid was."

"It could have been worse. It could have landed on you. And look at the opportunity it gave us to meet." He smiled. "Where are you from, Quinn Michaels?"

His eyes twinkled as he spoke, and Quinn took full notice of how handsome he was.

"I grew up in northern Vermont and live in New Hampshire. How about you?"

"Boston, born and raised." His eyes traveled to her lanyard. "Dartmouth, huh? That's impressive."

Quinn had checked out his lanyard when he sat down. "Not as impressive as Mass General. What's your specialty?"

Caden took a sip of his coffee. "I work in the Emergency Department. How about you?"

"I'm on the Med Surg wing. Can't imagine working the ED in a big city."

"It has its moments. My older sister lives in Hanover. She's on the accounting team at the hospital."

Quinn smiled. "Oh, she's one of those people who decides if we get a raise or not."

Caden chuckled. "I don't think she's that powerful, and I'd never let her know if she was." He took another sip of coffee. "But in any event, you'll be safe from her red pen slashing your budget because next month, she'll be going on parental leave. She and her husband are expecting a baby between Thanksgiving and Christmas. It's the first grandchild on both sides, and it's a boy. It'll be the first male in my family since I was born thirty-two years ago. In case you can't tell, it's a 'big deal.'" He did air quotes when he said "big deal," and Quinn laughed.

He grinned in response. "I'm serious! Just ask my mother."

"She's excited about a grandchild."

"Oh, you can't begin to imagine."

"Just you and the accountant to give them to her?"

"God no. I have three younger sisters. I grew up surrounded by strong doses of estrogen. How long have you been at Dartmouth?"

Quinn sensed he was fishing for her age. "I've been there two years. Went to school in Virginia, worked there for a year and then spent a few years in Seattle. I'm twenty-nine." She saw approval in his eyes when she mentioned her age.

"What brought you back to New England?"

"They recruited me. I was ready to leave Seattle, so I posted my résumé on a couple of job sites to see if there was any interest. Dartmouth contacted me within two days, did a phone interview, flew me east for an in-person interview, and then made a generous offer that I couldn't refuse. It's been a good move for me."

The speaker stepped to the podium, bringing an end to their chatting. Quinn settled back in her seat, slightly amazed at how easy the conversation had flowed between them. She rarely talked that much to someone she had just met. He was very attractive in his light-blue shirt, navy pants, and blue tie. All that blue made his eyes pop, and like Monday night, she was reminded that men at home didn't dress like that.

Quinn watched Caden taking notes even though they would have access to the PowerPoint slides. *Just like I do.* She liked that he took his commitment to being present seriously.

During a break between speakers, she asked him if he had been at the Healthy Living conference on Tuesday.

"I was. I remember you now. You were sitting about halfway up, and you smiled at me. Plus, you knew the woman I was sitting next to."

She blushed and said, "Yes, that was my friend Angie. I think I saw you at the lobby bar on Monday night too. Were you there?"

"Yes." He tilted his head, squinting his eyes as if he were thinking hard. "Were you wearing a purple sweater?"

She nodded.

"I only caught a quick glimpse of your face, but I remember you." He grinned at her. "I missed Tuesday afternoon and yesterday because of work pressures. And there's a good chance I won't make it back for tomorrow's sessions, even though I'm registered for both days."

Once the morning session ended, Caden asked, "Do you want to have lunch together?"

She felt her cheeks flush again as she smiled. "I'd like that."

They were talking as they left the conference hall, and Quinn didn't notice Sam waiting for her in the lobby until he called out, "Quinn! Hey, Quinn!"

She stopped. Sam had not crossed her mind all morning, and she forgot that they had agreed to meet for lunch. *Damn, this is going to be awkward.*

"Oh, hi," she said. "Why don't you join us? Caden, this is Sam Carpenter. We met at the other conference and rode here together. Sam, this is Caden Brady. Some kid knocked my drink out of my hand this morning, and Caden bought me a replacement."

Caden and Sam shook hands before they all continued toward the lunch buffet.

Sam

What the hell?

Sam noticed Quinn was more animated than she had been all week, and she invited him to join her and the guy at her side for lunch. Sam was sure he and Quinn had already made plans to eat lunch together. She made it sound like they had just met instead of acknowledging the long history they had. As they sat down, he glanced at Caden's lanyard and realized that he was a doctor at Mass General.

How am I going to compete with a doctor?

Shaking his head to clear his thoughts, he reminded himself that he wasn't competing with anyone for Quinn. That thought should not have entered his head. Caden seemed like a nice guy, friendly and outgoing.

Caden excused himself to go to the restroom, and Sam caught Quinn's eye. "Um, Quinn, didn't we have plans to have lunch together? You invited me to join you like... I don't know, like a stranger off the street."

At least she looked chagrined. "You're right, we did. I'm a little flustered."

"By the doctor?"

"Yeah. He's charming. He bought me that drink and was so easy to talk to. That doesn't happen to me every day."

Caden returned, and the three of them chatted comfortably while they ate. Sam noticed that Quinn seemed fascinated by every word Caden said, and he tried not to let it bother him.

When they all stood to return to the lecture halls, Sam asked Quinn, "Should we meet in the lobby for the ride back to Boston?"

She agreed, and they parted.

Chapter 15
Aurora

Quinn

As Caden and Quinn walked back to their conference room, Caden asked, "Is there something going on between you and Sam?"

She shook her head. "No. What makes you think that?"

"There was a vibe I picked up. Like he didn't think much of finding me with you. I was going to ask if you'd like to join me for dinner tonight, but I won't intrude if there's something between the two of you."

"We went to the same high school, hadn't seen each other in years, then ended up sitting next to each other on Monday. We've been catching up, but that's all it is."

"Well then, would you like to go to dinner?"

Damn. "I'd like that, but I made plans for dinner with Sam tonight. It'll probably be the last time we see each other for another ten years. I'm sorry." *I wish this wasn't my last night in Boston. I'd love to have dinner with Caden.*

They sat in the conference hall, chatting about their respective jobs. Quinn had done a six-week rotation in the Emergency Department during college, which she'd found overwhelming with the variety and volume of patients. Caden talked about different scenarios he'd experienced and ways his team kept their morale up.

"Do you have aspirations beyond your bachelor's degree in nursing?" he asked.

"I do. I'm working on my master's degree. In the spring, I'll be an Advanced Practice Registered Nurse."

"It's always good to keep advancing. I'm working toward a master's in hospital administration. Not sure I want to work in the ED my whole life."

They'd been talking for over twenty minutes when someone stepped to the podium to announce that the speaker could not attend and that the lectures would resume after the break.

Caden grinned at Quinn. "Do you want to walk around? We could explore the campus a little."

"I'm happy sitting here talking with you."

He gave her a warm look. "I'm fine with this too."

Just before the end of the break, he told her he'd be going to Hanover when his nephew was born. "Would you like to go to dinner while I'm up there? I can't spend all my time oohing and ahhing over the baby."

She smiled. "I'd like that."

"Can I have your phone number?"

She took his phone and entered her info while he did the same with hers.

The last speaker finished, and they prepared to leave. "I enjoyed today," Caden said. "I hope we'll be able to connect in Hanover."

"I enjoyed it too. For a day that started with a spilled chai, it turned out much better than I expected."

Sam

Sam joined Quinn at the entrance a few minutes after Caden left. As they settled into the backseat of the rideshare, Quinn leaned against him and sighed. "I'm exhausted."

The traffic was heavy, and as they slowly made their way back to Boston, Quinn closed her eyes and fell asleep in minutes. Sam enjoyed the weight of her head on his shoulder. It was the first time since he'd arrived in Boston that he was happy to be stuck in traffic. He was in no hurry to arrive at the hotel where he would have to wake her.

The driver remarked, "Long day? She's out like a light."

"We were in lectures all day," Sam answered. "Mentally exhausting."

"You're a lucky guy. I wouldn't mind having her on my shoulder."

They finally arrived at the hotel, and Sam whispered, "Quinn." She didn't respond, so he said, a little more forcefully, "Quinn, we're at the hotel."

Her eyes opened. "Oh my God, did I fall asleep?"

Sam grinned at her as she struggled to get herself together.

The driver turned around. "Nice having you in my car, Aurora," he said with a grin as Quinn blushed. Sam glanced at the driver with a question in his eyes. "My three daughters are obsessed with princesses. Sleeping Beauty is Aurora."

Quinn's blush deepened, and she said, "Well done. They should be proud of you." She looked at Sam. "God, that is so embarrassing. I didn't know I was that tired. I'm sorry."

"Don't apologize. I didn't mind at all. What time do we need to leave for dinner?"

"Our reservation is at six thirty. We should leave around six. I'll order a ride. Meet you here?"

"Sure, what are you going to do now? I'm going to call Piper to chat with her for a bit. Maybe you should take a nap." Grinning, he dodged the hand that reached out to swat him.

His bad dreams from the night before occupied Sam's thoughts before he called Piper. The main thread had been Norah keeping him from seeing Pip. Sam didn't believe Norah would try to keep him away from his daughter, but in the dreams, there was either a locked door between them or Norah had moved unreasonably far away.

The dreams shook him to his core, but he couldn't share all of that with Quinn. He'd dumped enough on her this week. *I need to get things settled with Norah as soon as possible. This uncertainty is killing me. I need to find a lawyer.*

He called Norah's phone, but it went to voicemail. "Hi, Pip. One more sleep until I'm home. I love you to the moon."

Once he ended the call, he stretched out on the bed.

Shit, I should have said two more sleeps. I'm never going to get this right.

Quinn

Quinn sat on the bed, rubbing her feet before stripping off the rest of her clothes and stepping into the shower. After the shower, she rubbed a citrus-scented lotion all over her body and then dressed in jeans, a black camisole, and a white shirt. She left her hair down and put on eye makeup, applying it more heavily than she had throughout the week.

With ten minutes to spare, she stood in front of the window, thinking about the day. Caden had been a pleasant surprise. He was attractive and interesting, and he oozed charm. *Is he as genuine as he seemed? I can't believe he brought me that drink. I've never had that happen outside of a bar. And man, is he hot—classically tall, dark, and handsome.*

His invitation to dinner had surprised her. *Damn, I would have loved to go to dinner with him, but I don't break plans with friends because a better offer comes along.*

She hoped he'd follow through on his promise to call when his sister's baby arrived. *Hmm.* Her moratorium on dating might actually come to an end, thanks to Caden. *He's the first guy that has piqued my interest. Maybe I am ready.*

Chapter 16
Quinn Confesses

Sam

THE HOST LED QUINN and Sam to a secluded table at the back
of the restaurant and gave them the dinner and drink menus.

While they were waiting for the server, Quinn asked, "Do
you have any pictures of your house? I'd like to see what you've
done."

Sam snickered. "Do I have pictures? You may regret asking
that. I could talk all day about the renovations." He picked up
his phone, opened an app, and handed it to Quinn. "They're
all in this album. There's before shots, the plans I drew,
work-in-progress pics, and then photos of the final product."

As she flipped through the images, Sam studied the menu,
trying not to care about her reaction.

"This is nice," she murmured. "You did an amazing job!
Hardwood floors?"

"Mostly. There's some tile as well."

"You did all of it? By yourself?"

"Jesse helped me with some things, and a friend from work. I know my limitations and hire subs for jobs I'm not qualified for, like the tile. But I did the bulk of it." He tried to act nonchalant, but a flush of satisfaction flowed over him. It was important to him that Quinn appreciated his work.

"And the way you've got everything put together in this album." She handed him back his phone. "I don't see anything scattered about this at all."

"Putting together visual stuff has always been easy for me."

"I remember my dad doing projects around the house. Renovations make a mess. How did Norah deal with that? You mentioned how she wants everything neat and tidy."

"She knew what we were taking on when we bought the house, so she was ready for it. The first room I did was the study. And then our bedroom. So she had two places that were her refuge. I'm glad you like it." He paused. "On a different subject, I love Italian food, but my usual restaurant is one with a more basic menu and all-you-can-eat breadsticks." He grinned sheepishly at her. "What are you going to have?"

"Can I order for you? It'll give me a chance to show off my Italian."

"You've learned Italian?"

Quinn laughed. "Not really, but I spent ten days in Italy last summer and became good at navigating the menus."

"No way. Who'd you go with?"

"I went by myself. I enjoy traveling, and it's tough to find someone with no commitments to go with me. I try to take a big vacation at least once a year."

"See, that's what I told you last night. Much more adventurous than I am. Where else have you been?"

"In addition to Italy, I've been to France, Germany, and Norway." She ticked them off on her fingers. "And then Colorado, New Mexico, and California. I loved northern Cali." As the server approached, she asked Sam, "A drink?"

He shook his head vehemently.

"I'm going to have a glass of wine. One glass," she emphasized. She ordered a glass of Moscato for herself and a San Pellegrino for Sam.

When the server returned with their drinks, he also brought warm bread and olive oil for dipping. "Are you ready to order?"

She ordered three items in Italian, only to have the server stare at her blankly. "Any chance you could repeat that in English?" She repeated the items in English, and Sam tried to hold in his laughter, which erupted as soon as the server walked away.

Quinn started laughing as well. "That's what I get for trying to show off."

Sam struggled to get his laughter under control and said, "Garlic shrimp, pasta carbonara, and penne beef sounded much sexier in Italian."

"I know, right?" Quinn tore off a chunk of bread and dipped it in the oil. "This is one of my weaknesses. We're going to have way too much food."

As Sam tore off a piece of bread, he asked, "You know what I thought about when you fell asleep on the drive?"

She rolled her eyes. "I can only imagine."

"The bus rides home after ski meets. You'd lean against me, and my eighteen-year-old self was in heaven the whole way home."

"I haven't thought about that in years. I fell asleep on some of those rides too. God, we were so young."

Sam nodded. "We were. So much time wasted."

"How so?"

"I wish we had truly gotten together during my senior year instead of only texting, hanging out at ski meets, and stealing a few minutes together during the school day." He frowned. "I let my parents have such an enormous influence on me, and they were adamant that you were too young for me to date. We could have had that entire year together instead of waiting until the next summer."

Quinn shook her head. "I understand where they were coming from. You were already eighteen—quote, legal age, unquote." She smiled. "I was only sixteen, and if we'd gone too far, you could have gotten into real trouble."

Sam nodded. "My father reminded me of that every chance he had. It makes sense now, but it certainly did not back then, when all I wanted to do was spend time with you."

"Remember our righteous indignation that they didn't trust us?" Quinn chortled. "There's nothing like teenagers who think they know everything."

"For the record, I'm never letting Piper date." Sam laughed, though, so Quinn knew he was only semiserious.

Her laughter faded in the wake of a rush of emotion, and Quinn placed her hand on Sam's arm. "Also, for the record, you were worth waiting for."

"I feel the same way about you."

The shrimp came, and Sam took the first bite. His face lit up, and Quinn smiled. "Delicious, huh?"

He nodded and took another bite. They continued to reminisce about ski meets while they waited for the rest of their food to arrive.

"I have a question," Sam eventually said. "You asked me on Monday why Norah and I aren't married. How about you? I always pictured you married with a couple of kids by now. When we broke up, you were in college with tons of guys around. I figured you'd find someone quickly. We've talked all about me, but you haven't told me anything about your dating life."

Quinn

Sam's question surprised her. She thought for a minute about how to answer. "I guess my priorities changed. As a teenager, I thought I'd be married by now, too, but it hasn't happened. And I'm okay with that."

"There's no one special in your life?"

"No." He'd been painfully honest with her, and she wanted to be the same. "Honestly, I spent my whole freshman year in college thinking that you and I would get back together."

She watched him frown, but before he spoke, she added, "Obviously, I gave up on that dream, and in my sophomore year, I started dating a guy who worked at the grocery store where I shopped. He was fun and asked little of me. We could only see each other on Monday and Thursday night." She ran her hand through her hair. "You and I were together all the time. I mean, when you weren't at college." She paused, staring down at the table. "I felt crowded by that, so someone who didn't want as much was ideal."

Sam's face flushed. "I thought you enjoyed being with me as much as I enjoyed being with you."

"I did! It's a contradiction. I loved being with you, but I wanted to be on my own too. We were so codependent."

Sam made a self-deprecating face. "Point taken. I tend to let that happen in my relationships. The therapist Norah and I went to pointed it out."

The server brought their food, and they both took a bite.

Quinn asked, "What do you think?"

Sam moaned. "This is great. You can order for me anytime. So, what happened to the grocery store guy?"

"My senior year, I had classes on Monday and Thursday night." She took a drink of her wine and then stared at her glass. "When I told him and suggested that we could get together on different nights or on the weekend, he flipped out. Accused me of not loving him and told me if I wanted to see him, I'd drop the classes. I refused, and he punched a hole in the wall." She paused, shaking her head. "All I could think was that it could have been me. I walked out the door and stopped responding to his calls or texts."

Why am I spilling my guts like this? I haven't even shared any of this with my closest friends. All I've told them is that I'd made some poor choices in who I dated.

She gazed at Sam and took a deep breath before continuing. "At the start of my last semester, he showed up at my apartment with flowers, asking if we could try again. He was available whenever I wanted, a total change from the prior two years. He's the reason I stayed in Richmond."

She twirled her fork through the pasta and lifted it to her mouth, chewing deliberately and then swallowing. "Six months after graduation, I opened my door to a woman wearing his engagement ring and holding a baby that looked like him." This was the worst part of the story. "Their relationship had started before we met and continued the whole time we were together, until she finally got fed up and left him, not knowing she was pregnant. The baby was born six months later, and she came back to give him one more chance. He told her I was out of the picture, and she was trying to verify his claim."

She concentrated on her meal but finished the story. "I ended it, but I had committed to the hospital for a year. I moved to Seattle as soon as that year was up." She quickly took another bite, not wanting to meet Sam's eyes.

"God, Quinn, that's terrible." Sam's voice was hushed.

She finally looked up. "Yeah, I was stupid. I swore it would be a new city and a new start in Seattle."

He nodded, and they ate in silence for a bit.

At one point, she reached into her pocket for a hair tie and pulled her hair into a ponytail. Then she saw Sam's knowing grin. "What? It's hot in here."

"You always had a hair tie. I can't believe you still carry one with you."

"I get hot!"

He shook his head, chuckling. "Okay. What happened in Seattle?"

She shrugged. "I played with online dating and gave up on it after I'd been there for a while. It's a waste of time if you're hoping for a long-term relationship. Ryan and I met at the gym. It was the most normal relationship I'd been in since, well, since you." She smiled a little. "Or so I thought. Everything was great for a while. But then he started demeaning me in little ways.

Nothing I did was ever quite good enough. My music choices were bad. I enjoyed the wrong movies."

She took a bite of her pasta and a swallow of wine. "At first it was subtle, but then it became more overt. Then it was all the time. I knew intellectually that I deserved to be treated better, but emotionally, I couldn't make the break. The final straw came during an argument when he shoved me. Shoved me hard. That was literally the push I needed. That night, I posted my résumé on some job sites, and the rest is history."

Sam pushed food around on his plate while Quinn was talking, watching her closely.

She continued, "I needed to figure out why I picked guys who were as far from you as possible, so when I started at Dartmouth, I found a therapist and swore off men. It took some time, but I finally realized I thought I didn't deserve someone who would treat me well. Both guys were losers in dead-end jobs. Grocery store guy didn't even graduate from high school. I figured if I rescued them, showed them a better life, they'd need me and wouldn't leave."

She drew a deep breath and blew it out. "That's the *Reader's Digest* version. It's more complicated than that, but you get the idea."

They had finished their meals, and Quinn asked for another glass of wine despite her earlier intention to have only one. She ordered tiramisu for them to share and concentrated on her breathing to quell the anxiety she felt from sharing so much, hoping her racing heart would slow.

Chapter 17
A Kiss

Sam

SAM WAS APPALLED AT what Quinn had told him. She'd been kindhearted and trusting when they were dating. How *could any man treat her that poorly?*

But was what I did any different? I didn't get physical with her, but I ripped her apart verbally.

"Quinn, I am so sorry you went through that, and for the way I treated you at the end."

She reached across the table, putting her hand on top of his. "Sam, I'm okay. I'm happy, incredibly happy. I love my job, and I have a circle of strong women as friends who would go to the mat for me. My home brings me joy, and I do what I want to do, like traveling. I genuinely love my life now."

"You truly haven't been on a date in two years?"

Quinn shook her head. "Nope." She dug her fork into the tiramisu and lifted it to her mouth as Sam continued to gaze at her. "Is it that hard for you to believe?"

"Do you get asked out? And say no?" Sam rubbed the back of his neck. "You can tell me if it's none of my business. I'm trying to picture what it would feel like to ask out a beautiful woman like you and be turned down."

Quinn laughed, and Sam knew it was because he was being so awkward.

She finally said, "I don't get asked out."

"That's hard to believe."

"I don't invite attention. I'm not approachable." She took a sip of her wine. "There are signs you give out. You meet someone's eyes, or you chat them up while standing at the bar. I don't do any of that. In my work environment, it's a known thing that Quinn doesn't date."

"You know a lot more about that process than I do. I drifted from you to Ginger to Norah. I've never really started from scratch."

"I'm aware." Sam could hear the sarcasm behind her words. "I had a lot of practice between grocery store guy and Ryan. I learned how to attract guys, and now I do the opposite."

"So two years and nothing? Not even one-night stands?"

"Sam!" He could hear the indignation in her voice. "That's inappropriate—and definitely none of your business!" She took another bite of the tiramisu. "You should try this, it's delicious. But to answer your question… No, not even one-night stands."

He stabbed a bite of the dessert and chewed it thoughtfully as he studied Quinn. "Can I tell you I'll miss sex if I go two years without a woman in my life?"

Quinn laughed. "My God. You'll survive, I promise." She laughed again, shaking her head. "There are ways to take care of that, you know."

Sam's face reddened, and Quinn laughed some more.

Her expression became more serious, and Quinn placed her elbow on the table, propping her chin on her hand. As she leaned in, Sam felt the laser focus of her eyes on his. Her voice was soft but pointed. "You know what I don't miss? I don't miss doing everything in my power to please a guy. Being lied to or dodging fists? More things I don't miss. I don't miss being told I'm a liar and can't be trusted. My mental health is worth far more than any romp in bed will ever be."

Sam bowed his head for a moment. He recognized her inclusion of some of the accusations he'd hurled at her ten years earlier. Looking up, he met Quinn's eyes again squarely. "I deserve that. I know what I said when we split was wrong, but I didn't realize how much damage it did to you. There are plenty of men out there who aren't pricks like I was or like those two you described were."

They gazed at each other, and Sam hoped Quinn could see the apology in his eyes. She drained her glass of wine, took a deep breath, and said, voice low, "You don't belong in the same league as them."

"It's a league of men that hurt you and ruined your self-esteem. I belong."

She finished her wine. "You did. But hearing the truth about that last night, hearing you apologize, has been good for me." She tapped her chest. "I've got a calmness in my soul that I didn't have before. So thank you."

He reached for her hand, and she let him hold it. "Thank you for listening to all my woes this week. It's been an immense help." He squeezed her hand. "Friends?"

Quinn chuckled. "Do you ask all your friends if they have one-night stands?"

"No, I reserve that for women I met when they fell into my arms at fifteen."

Quinn shook her head then said, "I know you're apprehensive about being alone, but you'll be surprised by the inner peace that comes from not having other people to worry about. And you'll never be totally alone because you have Piper."

"You're right. But I also know the risk is worth the reward. The failure of my relationship with Norah has knocked me back, but I wouldn't trade away the good parts of it. And I know that there will be a woman for me in the future. I hope you don't shut yourself off forever from sharing your life with someone."

Quinn smiled softly at him. "We're promoting two contradictory points of view."

Sam smiled back at her. "Seems like there should be middle ground we could agree on." He saw the server approaching.

Quinn saw too. "God, we've been here for over two hours. They probably want the table." Although Sam reached for the check, Quinn picked it up first. "This is my treat, remember."

Quinn

Quinn could still feel the warmth of Sam's hand on hers as they walked out of the restaurant. It was mild for early November, and the moon was almost full. "Why don't we walk back?" She pulled the elastic from her hair, allowing it to cascade over her shoulders.

Sam laughed. "Are you worried about falling asleep again?"

Quinn chuckled as she shook her head.

They hadn't walked far when she found herself admitting, softly, "I'm afraid."

He slid his arm over her shoulders, and she didn't pull away. "I get that," he said.

Neither of them said anything for a while as they walked, and to her surprise, Sam's closeness increased her feeling of calm.

God, it's been so long since I walked like this with someone.

Halfway back, they stopped by a church where a carillon played. As they stood listening, Sam turned and lowered his mouth to hers. Quinn sensed the question in his kiss and responded tentatively at first. They continued to kiss gently, both exploring the lips they had once known so well, until the chimes stopped.

Sam pulled away, eyes on hers, and Quinn smiled at him. They started walking again, with Sam pulling her closer. Her arm found its way around his waist.

The kiss had sent shockwaves through Quinn. She didn't know what to say, so she simply let him pull her closer as they walked.

Not ready to let the evening end, she changed direction and led him toward Beacon Hill. They walked by the state house and a park where the trees were bedecked with small white lights, creating a fairyland that appealed to her, and she pulled him to a stop.

As they gazed around them at the lights, Quinn turned to Sam, trailing her fingers along his cheek. He wrapped one arm around her and twined his other hand in her hair. She responded by running a finger over his lips before putting her hand on the back of his head to pull his mouth to hers.

Neither one of them knew how long they stood locked in the embrace and lost in their own world, kissing deeply as they held each other. Sam finally tried to detach himself from her, but she kept her hand on the back of his head and wouldn't let him.

Against her lips, he whispered, "One of these drivers is going to tell us to get a room." He pulled back again, and this time, she let him go.

They resumed walking hand in hand, fingers intertwined. Her mind was racing. His erection had been unmistakable as they clung to each other. The feeling from her body pressed against his had turned her on the same way it did Tuesday night. She remembered her mother's words about not letting lust overtake rational thought.

This isn't lust—it's longing. I want more of his warmth.

Sam

Sam wondered if Quinn was feeling the same spark of desire as him. Her kiss was hungry, and his erection had to be obvious, but she wasn't pulling away. *My need for her is overwhelming.*

The surroundings became familiar to him, and he realized they were almost back to the hotel. "I don't want this to end," he said, pulling her to a stop.

"Neither do I."

They came together and locked lips again, their heated touches alternating between tender and rough. His tongue explored her mouth, bringing forth a sigh.

With a gasp, she buried her head in his chest and gripped him tightly. "We can't stay out here all night. We should head into the hotel."

He put his fingers under her chin, gently lifting it until her eyes met his. "One more minute. Please." When his lips found hers again, the passion he knew they'd both been missing since they parted ten years earlier flowed between them.

Reluctantly, Sam ended the kiss, caressing Quinn's cheek, before his arm returned to her shoulder. Drawing her tightly to him, he nodded, and they walked into the hotel.

Chapter 18
A One Time Thing

Quinn

WHEN THEY STEPPED INTO the crowded elevator, Sam reached for the seventh-floor button, but Quinn put her hand over it to stop him. *Nope.* Her finger punched the button for her floor, and she edged closer to him.

Sam leaned over and whispered in her ear, "I'm not a horny eighteen-year-old who carries a condom in his wallet. I don't have anything."

She whispered back, "They're provided in the club-level rooms."

They both laughed.

The elevator emptied at the eighteenth floor. *Finally.* Quinn wrapped her arms around Sam, not wanting to be separated even for the brief seconds it would take to climb to the twenty-fifth floor.

By the time they left the elevator and reached her door, her hands were shaking, and she fumbled with the key card. He put his hand over hers and guided it in.

The door clicked shut behind them, and Sam followed her farther into the room. Quinn took off her coat, tossing it on a chair before turning back to him and tugging off his jacket as well. He drew her to him, and as her breasts pressed against his chest, she longed to feel his hands, his mouth, *anything* on them.

"I wasn't anticipating this when I invited you to dinner," she murmured.

Sam loosened his hold on her so he could see her face. "Neither was I. Not at all. But Quinn, right now, I want you more than you can imagine."

"I want you, too, but..." She hesitated.

Sam reached out his hand to stroke her hair. "This is for us. We both want it. I'm not making any promises, and I'm not expecting anything from you. We go in with our eyes open."

Her heart pounded in her chest. "This is a one-time thing. But... be gentle. It's been a while."

Sam gazed into her eyes. "Was I ever not?"

"No," she whispered.

His arms tightened, bringing her close again, kissing her lips before moving his mouth down her neck. She sighed as his tongue teased her ear, backing up and drawing them farther into the room. Closer to the bed.

They separated, and he reached toward the buttons of her shirt. "Okay?"

"Please…"

He slowly worked each button free from the bottom to the top. Quinn watched his fingers work, the anticipation intense.

When he finished, he eased her out of her top and stepped back to look at her. "I wondered what you had on under that shirt."

Reaching out, he touched the lace at the top of her camisole and let his fingers drift into the top of her bra, a light, feathery touch that made her nipples harden in response. He lowered his mouth to the lace, flicking his tongue over the skin of her cleavage.

He sighed. "You smell so good. Like orange blossoms."

Quinn ran her fingers through his hair, pulling his face closer. She loved this slow, deliberate Sam.

"Can I take this off?" he asked, fingering the camisole. When she nodded, he reached for the hem and gently pulled it over her head. Her black lace bra barely contained her fullness as she took a deep breath. She could see the bulge of his erection pressing at his zipper, and she watched him shake his head, knowing he was working to gain control of himself.

Finally, his fingers kneaded her breasts through the bra then worked one out of its lacy cup. He lowered his mouth and played his tongue over the nipple, which pebbled beneath his touch. Quinn's breath drew in sharply, and when he finally took the whole nipple in his mouth, she pressed forward into him. He sucked hard while fondling the lace on the other cup.

She took his face in her hands and kissed him deeply, then they sat on the bed while she unbuttoned his shirt, trying to be as tantalizingly slow as he had been. Her kisses traveled from his mouth down his neck then onto his chest. Her tongue teased his nipple.

He moaned. "My God, Quinn."

He released her other breast from the bra and stroked the fabric. "I love seeing you bursting out of this, and that black lace is so sexy. But are you comfortable?"

"I am, and it feels sexy."

He smiled. "So we'll leave it," he said, his voice husky with desire. Slowly he made his way from one breast to the other, alternatively sucking intensely and then gently, playing with her nipples.

Quinn lay back on the bed, savoring every second. Attention to her breasts was one thing she had longed for in her self-imposed exile from men. His kisses and nipple-play brought her to the verge of an orgasm several times. Her hand reached for his crotch, and when her fingers found his erection, a deep growl escaped his mouth. She stroked him, her pace as slow as that of his tongue moving on her breasts.

He worked his way down her stomach, planting kisses all the way to the top of her jeans and starting to unzip them before stopping abruptly. Quinn raised her head and watched as he slid from the bed to the floor. He unzipped her boots, pulled them off, and took her left foot in his hands, massaging it deeply.

"Oh my God." Quinn sat up. "You remember!"

He smiled at her, continuing to massage first one foot and then the other. Foot rubs had been one of her favorite things when they were dating, and she knew Sam enjoyed it as much as she did.

Squirming as her clit pulsed with desire, she was overcome by yearning to be filled with his cock. Her hands reached under his arms to pull him up to her, and as he stood, she unzipped his jeans, tugging at the waistband to slide them over his hips. Her breath caught. He was going commando these days, apparently, so pushing his jeans down left her facing his cock. His erect, larger-than-she-remembered cock. Her tongue snaked out to lick the head.

"Oh, Quinn," he said in that low, gravelly voice, which made her even hotter.

She opened her mouth and took him in, sucking hard at first then more gently, as he had done to her breasts.

His hands found the back of her head, pulling her closer. "I won't last long with you doing that." He moaned and thrust deeper into her mouth before taking a step back. "As much as I love your mouth on me, that isn't how I want this to end. I want to be inside you."

"I want that too," Quinn said. "These have got to go." She motioned toward his pants.

Sam kicked off his sneakers and stepped out of his jeans. Quinn inhaled deeply. He'd had a nice body ten years ago, but that had been the body of a boy. Now, he was undeniably a man with defined muscles and a well-developed cock standing out from the curly light-brown hair trailing down from his waist to his crotch.

Sam pulled her to her feet, unzipped her jeans, and slid them to the floor. Her black thong matched the bra, and Sam nudged her back so his gaze could run up and down her body. He reached out to caress her defined waist and then ran his hand down to her soft, round hips before lightly touching her breasts again.

"Different curves than I remember," he murmured. "You take my breath away."

"Mmm... I have a waist now."

Sam placed a finger over her mouth. "Stop that. I loved your body." His eyes ran over her again. "And I love it now."

They reached for each other, her breasts pressing into his chest and his erection fitting between her legs. They kissed deeply, tongues tangling and exploring again. His hand moved down to her thong and slid it to the floor before he lowered her to the bed, lying beside her and playing with her nipples again.

Quinn squirmed, desire driving every rational thought out of her mind. Her hand grasped his cock and stroked it from tip to base and back as his hand moved to her mound, seeking her clit. She twitched when he found it, a throaty groan escaping her mouth. He played there, working one finger and then two inside as she continued to stroke him and move against his hand.

He pulled his fingers out and lifted his head from her breast. "Quinn."

"I know." She moaned. "Are you as close as I am?"

He reached to stop her hand that was still stroking his erection, and she crawled over him to reach into the basket beside the bed, opening a foil packet and pulling the condom over his shaft before settling on top and lowering herself onto him.

She took him slowly, inch by inch. Her need to be filled was overwhelming, but the impulse to make this moment last was equally as strong. *He's as close to losing control as I am.*

Quinn knew Sam was struggling to stay still against her teasing slide onto him. He gazed into her eyes, murmuring, "You're killing me."

With a final slide, she took all of him and stopped moving, loving the fullness of him inside her. He didn't move, either, and seemed to be holding his breath, trying not to come too soon. Her breathing slowed, and her control increased. She gazed down at Sam, gauging the moment he stepped back from the edge as well.

Then she began to move, and her hands cupped her breasts, inviting him to touch. He reached up, tweaking her nipples, sending a shock wave through her body. A groan escaped as she started moving again and he thrust up against her gently. Pulling her down so his mouth could reach her breast, he sucked hard, and her excitement grew.

No more teasing. Her pace became steady, his cock sliding in and out of her. He continued sucking her nipples, and his thrusts became more aggressive. Blood pounded in her ears as a frenzy of pleasure overtook her, pushing her off the cliff. *"Sam!"*

Sam came a moment later, riding the waves wracking her body. She collapsed onto him, panting.

Sam

Holy shit.

Sam held Quinn until their breathing returned to normal then rose to take care of the condom. He caught his reflection in the bathroom mirror. He wasn't sure of the proper etiquette after mind-blowing sex with an ex following a ten-year hiatus, but he knew he didn't want to leave.

Quinn was at the bathroom door when he came out. She said, "I'll only be a minute."

Sam pulled a blanket off the bed, wrapping it around his waist as he walked to the window. He was gazing at the skyline when he heard her footsteps behind him and her body came up against his.

She embraced him from behind. "The city is stunning at night, huh?"

"Yes, it is." He turned, and his lips found hers.

Taking his hand, she drew him back to the bed and pulled him down with her, dragging the covers over them.

He sighed. "That was incredible. You're not a teenager anymore."

She snuggled against his shoulder. "We've both come a long way in ten years."

"You don't want me to leave?"

"No."

He turned toward her, embracing her fully in his arms. As his hands rubbed her back, contentment flowed through his body.

Quinn

Sam fell asleep first, and Quinn listened to his breathing, thinking about how amazing the sex had been. *Two years since I've been with a man, and God, it would be so easy to let this continue. And then I'd end up holding his hand while he extricates himself from Norah.* She didn't think she wanted to do that. But the thought of more mind-blowing orgasms made him very appealing.

Sleep didn't come easily as she weighed the pros and cons of letting this... whatever this was, continue. She silently laughed at herself. *I'm thinking about keeping this going while I have no idea how Sam feels. Maybe—hopefully—he knows, like I do, how shortsighted it would be for us to see each other again. To try to have a relationship. There is too much going on in his life to start something new.* She laughed again. *Or renew something old.*

Her fingers curled gently through his hair. *But it does feel good to be in his arms.*

Chapter 19
Sam's Conscience

Sam

SAM WOKE UP FIRST to find Quinn lying on her stomach with one arm draped across his chest. He lay there for a few minutes, savoring her closeness and thinking about how nice a repeat of the night before would be.

He gently said her name and nudged her shoulder. Her eyes fluttered open, and he said, "I need to go back to my room, get my stuff together, and schlep it to my car so I can check out before we go to Cambridge. And I need a shower."

"I have a late checkout and don't have to leave the room until four. You can bring your stuff here, then all you have to do this morning is check out. And when the conference finishes, you can grab your bag and head home." Her voice was still thick with sleep. She ran her fingers over his morning stubble. "I like this."

Sam grabbed her hand, brought it to his mouth, and nibbled her fingers, enjoying the way it made her shiver. There wasn't time for a repeat performance, but despite that practical thought, when a small moan escaped from her mouth, he hardened in response.

He ran his hand over her hair. "I wish we had more time."

"Yeah, me too. But I hate being late, so we need to get moving." Quinn sat up, wrapping the sheet around her, and watched as he scrambled to find his clothes.

Pausing at the door, he glanced back and said, "Can we talk later? About this?" He gestured between them. "Whatever this is?"

"That's a good idea. Take my key so you can get back in. It's there on the table."

Quinn

After Sam left, Quinn welcomed the water cascading over her in the shower as she remembered Sam's mouth and hands on her. They had both come a long way in ten years. Their lovemaking had never been like last night was.

Telling him about what a failure her relationships after him had been, combined with their conversation about her choice to distance herself from men, had shaken something in her resolve. His closeness on the walk back to the hotel had been comforting. And once they'd kissed, it was all over.

This can't be anything, she reminded herself. *There's a chance he and Norah will work things out.* Still, she was glad he wanted to talk about it.

She started repacking her suitcase. There was a soft knock at the door, and then Sam walked in with his backpack and a small duffle.

She stared. "That's all you brought?"

"Hey, I was only supposed to be here for two nights." They both laughed, and he walked over to the window. "I want to see this view in the daylight. It's impressive."

She blushed, remembering him almost naked in the same spot the night before. He wrapped one arm over her shoulders as he had on the walk back from the restaurant, and they kissed gently.

He groaned. "You look so nice. I don't want to mess up your makeup or your hair." He paused. "Actually, I do…"

Quinn completed the thought. "But we don't have time."

Traffic was heavy, and while they were on the road, Quinn's phone pinged.

> *Caden: Hey Quinn, it's Caden. I will not make it to the conference this morning. One of my PAs called out. I wanted to let you know again how much I enjoyed sitting with you yesterday and hope we'll be able to get together in Hanover. Hold on to your drink this morning!*

Her heart skipped a beat. Last night had driven all thoughts of the handsome doctor out of her head. Quinn smiled as she read his text and told Sam it was Caden.

"You liked him, huh?"

"He was nice. I enjoyed talking with him about his experience running an emergency department." She saw Sam's eyes narrow. "What's that look supposed to mean?"

"That there was a vibe between the two of you."

"Funny, he said the same thing about you and me. Maybe I have a vibe with everyone."

"Maybe you do."

The line at the coffee stand was short, so Quinn bought a chai on her way to the lecture hall. She took a selfie with it to include in her response to Caden.

> *Quinn: Drink intact. Sorry you can't make it today. I'll look forward to seeing you in Hanover.*

She paused before hitting Send. *Should I have said that? That I'm looking forward to seeing him? After last night?* Her finger hovered for a moment and then decisively punched the symbol to send the message on its way.

The speaker was interesting, but she had a tough time concentrating on what was being said. Memories of Sam and the night before filled her mind. She'd been surprised when Sam mentioned she had a vibe with Caden and hoped it wasn't motivated by jealousy.

What was I thinking when I told him to bring his bags to my room? They could have been left at the desk. She knew that. Maybe he didn't know, or maybe he did but wanted an excuse to return there with her. And maybe she wanted that too.

A replay of last night? The thought made her stomach jump and her center throb. *Yes, I want a replay. And then we talk.*

Am I making a big assumption, thinking that he'd want a repeat performance? No, he said enough this morning that I'm certain he wants more.

One last afternoon together, a final closure between them. Sam had work to do—he needed to learn how to be on his own. She would not get involved until his relationship with Norah was finished.

Quinn wondered how long that would take. It was impossible to know. She wanted to tell him to call her in three or six months, but there was no arbitrary time limit for recovering from heartbreak.

One thing I know is that I've missed that closeness. Maybe it's time to reenter the dating world. If Caden calls when he's in Hanover, I'll go out with him. She sighed. *Who am I kidding? He was just blowing smoke. Guys like that never follow through.*

Sam

Sam had always been easily distracted, but he found himself totally unfocused in his session. Not one thing the speaker said would stay with him, not when he couldn't stop remembering how Quinn's body had joined with his. The sex had never been like that in the time they were together. Hell, he wasn't sure he'd *ever* had sex like that. And he wanted more.

Then he thought, *Wait, I cheated on Norah.*

Fuck! Where did that come from? She walked away. I never cheated on Norah, never considered it. Even though we're not married, I took my commitment to her seriously. But now she's gone. She ended our life together.

He closed his eyes and rubbed his hand along his jaw. His conscience kept jabbing at him: *You never moved on this quickly. It was months after you met Ginger before you had sex with her. And you didn't rush into it with Norah either. It's only been* four days *since she moved out.*

He willed the thoughts to stop. *Quinn and I hadn't fully broken up when I met Ginger. That's why I waited. And Norah knew I needed to get over Ginger before going all-in with her.*

But you don't need to be fully disentangled from Norah before getting it on with Quinn?

He shook his head as if to rid it of doubt. *No! Jesus, things have been going south with Norah for so long. We're not coming back from this.*

He and Quinn had both been needy the night before. Hungry for connection and warmth. And for closure. Having sex with Quinn felt like the final step in healing and closure for both of them.

But I don't want it to be the final step. I want more—and not only sex. I love being around her.

His conscience chimed in again. *What if there is something between her and the doc? She appeared damn happy at receiving the text from him. He has way more to offer her than you do. She deserves the chance to see if that was more than a vibe.*

He mentally groaned. *Shut up! Just shut up! I have no idea what Quinn wants, but we said we would talk, and I'm going to lay my cards on the table. The only thing I know for sure is that whatever happens when we leave here, I will not hurt her again.*

At noon, they climbed into the car for the ride back to Boston, and Sam put his arm on the seat back.

Quinn leaned into him and said, "I'm not falling asleep today."

He laughed and snaked his hand under her jacket onto her thigh, which led her to snuggle in more closely. His hand drifted toward the V of her legs, and she didn't stop him. He gently stroked her through the cloth, which brought forth a soft sigh that he was sure only he could hear. She put her hand over his to increase the pressure, and his cock jumped to attention as his conscience finally quieted down.

Traffic was light, however, and the ride was over more quickly than either of them wanted.

Chapter 20
Passion Explodes

Sam

Quinn fumbled with the key card again, and Sam took it from her to open the door. As soon as they stepped into the room, they wrapped their arms around each other, mouths melding together, tongues twining.

She tugged at his coat. "Too much clothing!"

He tore off his jacket, and she did the same. Grabbing the hem of her sweater, he pulled it over her head and dropped his mouth to her chest, pushing her bra out of the way to reach one nipple. Moaning, she pressed against him. He paused, scooped her up, and carried her to the bed, leaving her legs dangling over the edge. Reclining next to her, he took one nipple in his mouth again, running his fingers over her other breast. Her hand reached for his zipper.

"Wait," he said. "Let me play a little." When her eyes questioned him, he smiled. "Relax."

"Relax? I feel like I'm about to explode!"

Sam cupped her cheeks with both hands and kissed her deeply. She sucked on his tongue, arching her body into his. He drew her into a tight embrace, one hand on her back while the other slid between her legs. One of her hands moved toward his zipper again, and he batted it away as he planted kisses all the way to the top of her leggings.

He slipped off the bed, kneeling at her feet the same as the night before. His hands massaged her bare feet even more deeply. *Does this qualify as a foot fetish?* Whether it did or not, it was making him hotter and harder. Quinn's squirming told him he was stirring up equally as much desire in her.

Finally, he pulled off her leggings and thong and began kissing his way up her legs. His hand reached up to her wetness where his fingers became lost in the folds.

"Oh my God, you're killing me," she whispered.

One finger slid inside, then another. His mouth reached her thigh, still kissing all the way, and then he buried his head between her legs, flicking his tongue against her sweet spot.

Quinn lifted her mound, moving against his mouth, making little whimpering sounds as she squirmed. His fingers plunged deeper into her.

"Sam," she moaned, "I'm not going to last."

"That's okay. Let go, baby. Let yourself come."

His fingers moved in and out of her heat as his tongue circled her clit. Her legs tightened around his head as she orgasmed in waves that left her gasping.

When the spasms wracking her slowed down, he slowly withdrew his fingers and crawled up beside her on the bed, wrapping his arms around her as her breathing returned to normal. Her lips sought his, and Sam wondered what she thought, tasting herself on his mouth.

He was hard as a rock, beyond ready to continue.

Quinn reached her hand to his crotch and rubbed against his erection. "That was incredible, but it left you high and dry."

"Oh, I got plenty. Feeling you come like that was something."

Shifting her position, she unbuttoned his shirt and laid her head against his bare chest. Her mouth found one of his nipples and sucked gently on it. Sam moaned and lost his fingers in her hair. Her hand snaked into his jeans and found his cock straining to be free.

She pulled herself away from his chest and unzipped his pants, which he promptly kicked off. Sitting up to finish taking his shirt off, he reached over to unhook her bra. Much like the night before, his gaze studied her from head to toe.

"You are so beautiful," he said, his voice thick.

Their lips met, and despite his overwhelming need to be inside her, he took his time exploring her mouth, savoring the sensations as his hands roamed her body. Her nipples pebbled in response to his touch.

Quinn sighed and pushed him down onto the mattress. Lying next to him, she took him in her hand, stroking from tip to bottom while her other hand grabbed his and guided it back to her center. He moaned and stroked her gently as she squirmed against him again, little sighs escaping her lips.

"Quinn. I want to be inside you."

"I want that too. The condoms are in the basket beside the bed."

Sam tore one open, covered his shaft, and lifted himself over her, then touched her again to be sure she was ready for him. Sucking on her breast yielded exactly the reaction he was hoping for, soft moans and more squirming. He rubbed his erection into the wetness between her legs, moving it back and forth, increasing the desire and tension for them both. Quinn was breathing hard and raising her mound in response.

Finally, he slid his cock slowly inside until it was buried to the hilt. He stopped, savoring her heat, while she slid her hands down to his butt, trying to pull him in more deeply.

They kissed, and he raised one hand, flicking one of her nipples, which was swollen and hard. He hoped she could feel him throbbing.

When he began to move, she rose to meet him. They established a rhythm—slow, then fast, then slow again—that took them close to the edge over and over. Twice he stopped altogether, leaving his shaft buried in her while he struggled to regain control. Then he knew it was time. He moved again, stroking steadily, then he put his hand between them to reach her clit. That extra pressure was all she needed.

She cried out, coaxing him to move faster. "Oh God, don't stop again. I need this!" Her climax hit, stilling her movements as she closed her eyes, and Sam's followed seconds later. Wave after wave of pleasure held both of them in its grasp.

With a deep exhale, she went limp beneath him as he collapsed onto her. After a second, he rolled so that they were side by side. Gradually, their heartbeats returned to normal.

Eventually, he climbed off the bed to take care of the condom and returned to find her under the covers. Crawling in to join her, he wrapped his arms around her. She turned to him, running her tongue over his bottom lip and teasing his mouth open. He moaned softly as her tongue explored his. *God, there's as much desire between us now as there was before.*

His hands gently caressed her back as he confessed, "I couldn't tell you one thing that was said in my session. All I could think about was last night."

Quinn

"Same for me." Quinn's hand drifted down Sam's back, stopping to fondle his butt. Gazing into his eyes she whispered, "I embarrassed you last night when I said there's ways to take care of the lack of sex."

He grimaced. "Noooo."

Quinn smiled. "You blushed."

Sam's face reddened again, and Quinn knew his cock had jumped to attention.

Then he said, "I need a lesson."

"Hmm?" Her head tilted inquisitively toward his.

"Touch yourself. Let me watch."

Quinn hesitated before reaching between her legs, and Sam pushed the blankets away so that he could see. Her fingers made tight, slow circles over her folds, and she sighed.

"All on the outside?" he asked, voice husky.

"Mostly."

"Only your fingers?"

"I have vibrators at home." Her fingers continued making tight circles, and Quinn felt his erection grow against her thigh. "I wasn't expecting anything like this when I packed for the week."

He laughed. "Neither was I." He cupped her breast and started tracing circles around her nipple. A small moan escaped from her mouth in response. "My God, watching you is so hot. Did you do this Tuesday night?"

She grinned. "What do you think?"

"I wish I'd been there instead of passed out on my bed." He wrapped himself more tightly around her, the erection pressing into her hip adding to her excitement.

She squirmed against her hand, increasing the pressure. "I'm not sure I'll come. I've never done this with someone watching."

He pinched her nipple. She drew in a sharp breath and jumped slightly.

"You are so gorgeous, Quinn. I'm so turned on. I can feel the heat flowing off you. Let go. I want to see it happen." He rose on one elbow to lower his mouth to her breast. His tongue took the place of his fingers, tracing circles around one nipple.

She moaned, moving faster and pressing harder, shifting her hips, trying to hit her sweet spot. Breathing hard, she sighed, slowed her fingers, and looked at Sam. "Almost there, but then I lost it. That happens sometimes."

"And what do you do then?"

Her whole body was still on fire, but her face flushed hotter as she smiled at him. "Keep trying."

His grin said it all. "Please do." He reached to put his hand over hers, matching her pace for a few minutes before returning to her nipples.

She felt the waves rising again, and this time, she put Sam out of her mind, concentrating instead on the sensations cruising through her body. Her voice low, she moaned, "Oh... oh... oh my God."

She could feel Sam watching her face as it contorted with pleasure when the orgasm hit her.

"Damn, Quinn. That was so hot."

As the waves wracking her body subsided, she turned toward him, grasping his cock and stroking it while she pulled his mouth back to her breast.

He teased his tongue gently over the nipple before asking with a smile, "More?"

She smiled. "That's something I've missed a lot."

His lovemaking turned aggressive, and Quinn met him with the same ferociousness, touching every part of his body before returning to his cock. He grabbed her hair and pulled her head back. They kissed passionately until Quinn broke away to reach into the basket by the bed. She tore open the package with shaking hands and pulled the condom over his erection before raining kisses over his body in a frenzy, ending up back at his mouth.

He knelt over her, rubbing his shaft between her legs, but that didn't satisfy her desire.

"Now, please. I want you so much."

He drove into her, and she rose to meet him. "Not slow, not this time," she demanded. "Show me how much you want me."

Sam pounded into her, meeting her upward thrusts with all he had. She panted for breath and exploded with a moan.

An intense orgasm overtook him a few seconds later. "Quinn... oh, Quinn. Oh my God." Holding tightly to her, breathless, he murmured, "I'm never going to let go of you."

Quinn was lying in the same position on Sam's return from the bathroom. He lay down next to her, leaned on his elbow, and propped his head on his hand. Gently stroking her hair, he gazed at her, shaking his head. His voice was full of wonder when he asked, "What was that?"

Quinn smiled. "The aftermath of a two-year hiatus? Incredible? Amazing?" She sighed. "Thank you."

"God, there's no need to thank me. I enjoyed it all as much as you did." He shook his head. "You're the most sensuous woman I've ever met. The girl I knew ten years ago has grown into an incredible woman—in every way. I never imagined you this independent, this adventurous." He grinned at her and ran a finger over her lips. "And this sexy. I can't wait until the next time."

She tilted her head and grinned back at him. "You think there's going to be a next time?"

Chapter 21
Leaving the Bubble

Sam

SAM'S STOMACH TWISTED AT her words. "I'd like there to be."

"I told you last night it was a one-time thing."

His eyebrows raised. "I think we're several times beyond one."

Quinn smiled, looking a little sheepish. "Remember who you're talking to. The woman who voluntarily banished men from her life. Have I said anything to make you think I've changed my mind about that?"

"You know how they say actions speak louder than words? Your actions spoke loudly."

Quinn pushed up to a sitting position and adjusted the sheet to cover her. "What about Norah?"

Sam rolled off the bed and walked to the mini fridge, where he grabbed two bottles of water. He gave one to Quinn before taking a long drink from the other and crawling onto the bed beside her.

"I was angry on the drive here. Angry that Norah was taking this step, and for the way she told me. I spent my entire time on the road trying to figure out how I could get her to come back." He took another long drink. "After I went for that run the first day, I called to talk to Piper and ended up talking to Norah as well. Her voice was as ice-cold as it had been that morning, and she made a sarcastic crack about me being on time."

Quinn frowned at him, and he knew she wondered what the big deal was about the sarcasm. "I know, I know—that doesn't sound like a big deal and I'm a big boy, I should be able to handle something like that. And I can." He waved his hand to emphasize his point. "But it hit me that we've reached the end of the road. We're not good for each other anymore. I don't like the person she's become, and obviously she doesn't like the person I've become."

Sam took another swallow from the water bottle and put it on the bedside table. He turned to Quinn and reached for her hand. "But you know the biggest thing I realized? The way she's acting, the coldness, that's not really Norah. She was never what I'd call sweet, but she's a kind woman, and being with me the last couple of years has driven that out of her."

"It can't be all your fault. She has control over how she acts."

Sam let go of Quinn's hand and rubbed his jaw. "It's us together. Let me ask you something. In the time we knew each other, a year of friendship and two years of dating, how often did you see me angry?"

"Just that last night."

"Right. You and I had our little arguments, but I never felt red-hot anger at you. And I told you I've changed, and that's one part of me that's changed for the worse. Until recently, I was always able to keep anger from controlling me because of what I saw from my father. And now... I'm angry all the time." He sighed. "Everything Norah does makes me angry, and everything I do brings out this shrew in her. I don't want to live like this, and I know Norah doesn't either. It doesn't feel good inside." He tapped his chest.

He turned and gazed out the window. "And most of all, I can't let things continue the way they have been because it's causing such emotional distress for Pip. You heard her stuttering! I can't keep contributing to that."

"From the way you talked Tuesday night, I would have sworn that you wanted Norah back."

"I'm sure I told you I'd realized Norah and I had reached the end. But I'll admit I was still reeling at that point. I've regained my equilibrium this week."

"I have to be honest with you." Quinn hesitated. "I feel like I have something to do with your decision."

"I was surprised and happy to see you on Monday. But I came to the conclusion about my relationship with Norah before we went out to dinner that night. And you know what I was doing yesterday afternoon, before the Italian restaurant and before this?" Sam motioned between them. "I was searching online for a lawyer. I have a couple I'm going to call on Monday. I had no idea you and I were going to end up in bed."

"Neither did I," Quinn admitted.

"I don't want to talk any more about Norah. I want to talk about us."

"There is no us."

"There could be." Sam reached for Quinn's hand again.

She let him take it, but she said, "I'm not looking for a relationship."

"Did I say anything about a relationship? Now that we've reconnected, I'd like to spend time with you. We don't have to define it."

"What? You want me to be your fuck buddy?" Quinn snatched her hand away.

"No. God no, that's not what I want. I just... I meant it wouldn't be like when we were teenagers. We talked about codependency. I don't want that." Sam took a long swallow from the water bottle. "Don't think I expect to spend all my time with you. Piper will be with me, and as much as I'd like you to meet her, that won't be for a while. I'm not throwing anything else her way that will confuse her."

"Have you thought about when you'll have her?"

"I want her half the time. I'm going to propose to Norah that I have her every other weekend and Monday and Tuesday nights."

"Do you think she'll agree?"

Sam shrugged. "I'll have to figure that out. But back to us."

Quinn shook her head.

"Don't you think that it's a bit of serendipity that we live so close to each other?" he asked. "Or that I ended up sitting next to you on Monday?"

She laughed. "You mean like we're meant to be?"

"I don't know about being meant to be, but I feel like this is a second chance. I was stupid ten years ago."

Quinn stood up, wrapped herself in the blanket, and walked toward the window. Sam started to follow until her hand went up, signaling him to stop.

"Give me a minute." She stood with her back to him. "We're not the same people we were back then."

"I know that. I want to get to know who you are now. And I want you to get to know me." He watched her and hardened again as he thought about Quinn's body under the blanket. He adjusted the sheet to make sure he was covered.

Damn, I've never wanted any woman as much as I want her. What will I do if she says this is it? That she never wants to see me again?

I'll have no choice. I'll continue to be the best dad I can to Piper, and I'll learn to be alone, like Quinn and I talked about.

He could do that. If he had to.

Quinn

Quinn stood at the window, thinking about the week. It had been surprising, emotional, enjoyable, and filled with passion. It wasn't only the emotional closeness with someone that was missing from her life, it was also the wild, sexual abandon.

These two years have been good for me. I know who I am now and what I want. I don't think I'll ever let myself be a doormat again. What the hell should I do?

She thought back to the years after their breakup. *A second chance with him is what I dreamed about for such a long time. Even when I was trying to convince myself that I hated him, there was always a tiny kernel of hope in the back of my mind.* The opportunity for closure... It wasn't easy to dismiss, despite her fears.

After a moment, she turned to him. "You know, we've been insulated here. It hasn't been real life."

Sam softly blew out a long breath. "I know that."

Quinn nodded. Her thoughts continued to spin. *Do I want to get involved with another needy guy? How needy is he? From what he said, it seems like he's started to make some plans. He knows Piper shouldn't meet someone he's dating right away, and he's thought about what a visitation schedule could be. I need to remember he's not the same immature boy I knew before.* She shook her head, trying to clear her thoughts.

When it comes down to it, what I am going to regret most if I say no? What am I going to miss—the sex or the person?

Finally, she walked back to the bed and sat on the edge. "I'd like to get to know the man you are now."

Sam broke into a wide smile. "You mean you'll spend time with me?" He reached down to adjust the sheet again, and Quinn could tell his cock had jumped to attention.

Glancing pointedly at his erection, she said, "Really, Sam? Already?"

He cocked his head. "You were ready for several encores a bit ago. But ignore that. It'll calm down. So, you'll see me back home?"

"Yes."

"Why do I feel you have conditions?"

"I don't think of them as conditions." She ran her hand through her hair, which caused the blanket to drop below her breasts.

"That's not helping to calm me down."

She pulled the blanket back up and grinned. "Sorry about that. I want us going into this with our eyes wide open, like you said last night."

He nodded.

"And if either of us decides it's not working for them, we let the other know and end it without recriminations. I won't go through another breakup like our original one."

"It feels like you're planning a way out before we even start."

"I could say take it or leave it."

Sam rubbed his jaw. "I know you could. It's your decision. I'd like to tease and beg, but I won't do that."

"I want us to be honest with each other about how we feel without worrying about being attacked."

His eyes clouded. "I guess I deserve that."

"Sam, I don't know how this will go, and neither do you. It's a big step for me to open myself up to the possibility of a relationship. There's a part of me that is scared." She reached over and put her hand on his leg. "But there's a bigger part that wants to spend more time with you."

Sam put his hand over hers. "I'm glad. And I agree with everything you've said."

"One more thing."

"What?" His voice sounded nervous.

"It's nothing bad. I want us to always be friends, even if we go in different directions. I've missed your friendship, Sam. I don't want to lose it again." Her eyes filled with tears.

Sam crawled over the bed so he could gather her into his arms. His voice was husky with emotion when he murmured, "I've missed that too."

They clung to each other for several minutes until Quinn sighed. "It's getting close to my checkout time."

Sam kissed her. "I know, and I need to shop when I get back to Vermont, so I'm ready for Piper." He climbed off the bed, slower than usual, and started getting dressed. Picking up his jacket, he gazed longingly at her.

She walked into his arms with the blanket still wrapped around her.

"I'll have Pip until Wednesday morning," he said. "Can we get together that night?"

"That works for me." She relished the warmth of their embrace. "We can text to make plans. I hope you don't get stuck in traffic."

"It can't be as bad as Monday was. I'll be in touch." He kissed her then turned back when he reached the door. "I'll see you in Vermont."

He'll see me in Vermont. I like the sound of that.

Quinn sat on the edge of the bed, processing everything, hoping their agreement to spend time together wasn't a mistake.

This week had changed so much for her. Breaking her self-imposed moratorium on dating hadn't been on her radar when she left Lebanon, but her body had betrayed her with Sam, showing her how much she craved the closeness and the sex. She couldn't get enough of him, and had there been time, she would have liked even more.

Where the hell did that come from? I've never been like that with a man.

More importantly, Quinn liked what he said about getting to know each other; she wanted that just as much.

Glancing at her phone, she realized the time and scrambled to the bathroom. A quick shower sufficed, and while pulling on her clothes, her reflection in the mirror caught her eye. *I look thoroughly ravished.* She smiled as her core heated again with the memory of Sam's touch.

After one last glance out the window, Quinn made her way to the registration desk and checked out. She paused before stepping onto the elevator to the parking garage to send a text to Angie.

Quinn: Going to see Sam back in Vermont. Never thought I'd agree to be his exit strategy. I'll tell you all about it when I see you in January.

The End

Chapter 22
Epilogue

Sam

Sam tapped his brakes as the traffic ground to a halt on the highway leading out of Boston. "Shades of Monday morning," he sighed, but even this delay couldn't spoil his good mood. The last few hours with Quinn had been unbelievable. As his car inched along, he remembered the feel of her smooth skin against his and the sensuality of watching her pleasure herself. Their time together should have sated his desire, but he hardened just from the memory of her. Finally, the traffic eased, and Sam increased his speed.

His phone pinged, and a reminder popped up on the car's media screen. Piper was invited to a pizza party to celebrate a classmate's birthday. The message brought him back to life in Vermont, and his thoughts drifted to Norah as the miles clicked by, Sam journeyed all the way back to their beginning.

As an unsophisticated twenty-three-year-old, Sam had shared an office with Jesse. Late on a Friday afternoon, Jesse had said, "That ANR lady is interested in you."

"Yeah, right," Sam had responded sarcastically.

Jesse had been knee-deep in a PhD program and had been open about his plans to strike out on his own as a workforce consultant. But on this Friday, over eight years earlier, he was working at the Upper Valley Economic Council and had taken Sam under his wing. Their current job bordered sensitive wetlands, and a woman from the Agency of Natural Resources had been dispatched to make sure they were respecting the boundaries. She had introduced herself as Norah Taylor and was due to make her fourth visit that afternoon. Jesse was the project manager on the job and communication with Norah went through him. "No, I'm serious. She asked if you were going to be there today."

Sam shook his head. "You're so enlightened, calling her a lady instead of a chick, or a broad."

"All those courses I'm taking on gender sensitivity, diversity and inclusion are paying off."

Sam chuckled. "Don't do any of that consciousness-raising voodoo on me." Then he scoffed. "I can't imagine why Norah would be interested in me. I'm low man on the totem pole." He had only been on the job for six months, and this was his second project.

"Exactly." Jesse grinned at him. "No offense, but your presence is not a necessity, and yet she wants you there. And she scheduled the meeting at four. Who does a meeting at that hour on a Friday? She knows we go out for drinks after work and will angle to come along. She's hot for you."

"Yeah, well, I'm not really available." Sam had moved in with Ginger right after he broke up with Quinn. Recently, she had started dropping hints about marriage, pushing him for a commitment he wasn't ready to give. He was becoming more and more aware that he never would be, not with Ginger.

"I thought you were going to move out."

Sam rubbed his neck. "That takes money, which I don't have."

"When are you going to get yourself together? The Ginger situation is toxic."

"I didn't spend years getting rich as a pro baseball player."

Jesse muttered something in Spanish and pushed back his chair to stand. "At least all your limbs are in working order." He limped toward the door. "Let's go. We don't want to keep the ANR lady waiting." He tossed Sam the keys to the company truck. "You can drive."

"What did the doc say about your knee?"

"More surgery." Jesse was curt and left no room for the conversation to continue.

They arrived at the construction site just in time to be brought up to speed by the crew leader. As the other men were leaving, a silver Lexus pulled into the lot. Sam watched, with Jesse's words, *"She's hot for you"* bouncing around his head, as Norah Taylor climbed out.

She was slightly shorter than Sam, with honey blond hair that she wore long and loosely cascading over her shoulders. It was unusually hot for late August and Sam appreciated the view of her legs in a short red skirt. She'd topped it with a black tank top that left nothing to his imagination.

"Hey Jesse, Sam. Let's check out how close that fence is to the wetlands border." Norah was all business the same as she had been at their prior meetings. She hardly looked at Sam, intent on inspecting the fence that had been erected.

Jesse definitely read that wrong. She is pretty, though. Sam had noticed that at their very first meeting.

Norah walked up and down the western border, and after several minutes she said, "You need to extend this fence by eight feet. We want to be sure that none of the construction debris encroaches on the wetlands." She looked expectantly at Jesse.

"We can do that, Ma'am if you think it's necessary." Sam knew Jesse was seething at the added expense to the project. The area Norah wanted fenced off was in the far back corner of the property and unlikely to be compromised by any aspect of the construction. "I'll send you a picture when we get it done."

"That won't be necessary." Norah swung her gaze between the two men. "I'll come back out to inspect it."

"Whatever works for you." Jesse looked over at Sam with a grin and raised eyebrows. "Is there anything else you want to look at?"

"I want to walk the perimeter." Norah turned back toward her car. "Just let me change my shoes." She opened the door and sat on the back seat with her feet on the ground.

Sam watched as she eased off one black high-heeled sandal and reached into the back of the car. She turned to face them, clutching a pair of white sneakers. He enjoyed the view of the gap inside her shirt, as Norah bent over to tie one shoe, kicked off the other sandal and pulled the second sneaker on. When she finished, she stood, bent to pick up the shoes, and tossed them into the back seat.

"I'm ready now." She dazzled Sam with her smile.

The property was over two acres of gently undulating farmland littered with divots ready to ensnare even the most physically fit person. Norah had turned to walk in the opposite direction and Jesse grimaced at Sam who knew the walk would be a problem for him. "How about if I walk it with you? We'll let the old man rest in the shade."

"Jesus." Jesse glared and muttered in Spanish again as Sam and Norah headed for the back edge of the property.

"Jesse's not that old, is he? I noticed the limp."

"Thirty-two, nine years older than I am." Sam was sure Norah was older than him and he wasn't going to hide his age. "He played professional baseball for Tampa Bay and tore his knee up in a collision at home plate. Ended his career." Turning the conversation away from Jesse, he said, "Nice car you drive."

Norah laughed, a gentle rippling sound that Sam found appealing. "It was a college graduation present from my parents. It's a little flashy for Vermont. That was four years ago. I hoped as it aged, it wouldn't stand out so much."

I wonder if my parents even realize I graduated. Sam buried that, as he always did thoughts of his family. He liked the way Norah had subtly told him her age. *She must be twenty-six. Jesse is reading her so wrong.*

It was close to five when they got back to Jesse, who was finishing a conversation on his phone. "Caitlin is going to meet us at the Sidecar. She dropped me off at work this morning, so we'll leave the work truck back at the office and take your car to White River." Jesse's eyes sparked at Sam. "Would you like to join us, Norah? We gather there to decompress from the week. Cait's my wife. She needs a break even more than the rest of us after caring for our two tiny humans."

Sam watched Norah's reaction to Jesse's invitation. Her eyes held him for a few seconds and then moved back to Jesse.

"I'd like that. By Friday afternoon, I'm toast."

Sam had grown to enjoy the Friday nights at the Sidecar with Jesse and other colleagues. There were pool tables which took him back to the Whistle Stop where he'd met Ginger after Quinn left for college. He still had only two beers, no matter how long they stayed. Trent Carpenter's shadow continued to loom long over him.

Talk around the table quickly turned personal and Norah shared that she'd recently ended a relationship. Jesse, aided by a couple shots of bourbon, had said, "Sam needs to do that. He's got a girl clinging to him like a barnacle on a boat and he can't get free."

"I told you," Sam mumbled. "Finances. I don't have the money to get my own place."

"How much do you need?" Norah looked at him seriously.

"Much more than I have, since my bank account falls to zero just before every payday."

Norah cocked her head. "Are you through with that girl?"

"I want to be."

"What he's not telling you," Jesse had had just enough alcohol to not know when to keep his mouth shut, "Is that he's still pining for the girl who broke his heart a few years back. The sweet Quinn."

Norah looked at him with a question in her eyes. "I gather she ended the relationship?"

Sam squirmed in his chair. "Not exactly. I'm not pining for her." He glared at Jesse, who grinned back, enjoying the exchange. "But there are things I said that I wish I could take back. Water over the bridge at this point."

Sam and Norah exchanged cell numbers before she left the Sidecar, and she started texting him tips on how to set up a budget and what the benefits would be. His parents had lived paycheck to paycheck, and no one had ever pointed out the things that Norah did.

Two weeks later, when Norah came to look at the new fencing, Jesse let Sam go by himself to meet with her. It was late on Friday again and the job site was vacant. As they walked the perimeter, Sam told her what he'd implemented of the strategies she'd given him. "The biggest step I've taken--I moved out of Ginger's apartment. I'm bunking in on a friend's couch. You were right. I feel so much lighter to be out of that situation."

"What's next? Are you going to get in touch with 'Sweet Quinn'?"

"No."

Norah remained silent for the rest of the walk, and Sam had suspected she didn't believe him.

Traffic ground to a halt, and Sam could see red and blue lights flashing on the road ahead. He groaned, wondering how long he'd be stopped because he needed to shop before getting to his house. That walk, eight years earlier, with Norah continued to bump against his psyche. *What she didn't know was that*

I'd already sought out Quinn. I'd never admitted that to anyone until I told Quinn Tuesday night. Not even Jesse knows that.

Traffic began moving, and Sam returned to ruminating about his early days with Norah. After it had become obvious, he wasn't going to hear from Quinn, Sam had invited Norah to dinner. After dinner, she had led him to her apartment, where they kissed for the first time.

A month later, Sam had moved in with her, and they proceeded to have sex on every piece of furniture Norah owned. He'd never been so sexually satisfied and had been amazed that Norah, who was better educated, better traveled, and more cultured than he would ever be, seemed to be just as fulfilled by him.

She took him to Connecticut to meet her family and Sam had been blown away by the size of their house. A feeling of inadequacy that he'd been fighting against began to creep in. *That house could have held three of my parent's home. Mitzi was friendly enough to me, but I knew she didn't think I was good enough for her daughter. I ignored so many red flags.* He remembered waiting for Norah to come to her senses and end it with him.

His gas gauge pinged, and Sam exited, shaking his head. The memories were so intense, he'd ignored his need for fuel. As Sam resumed the trek north, they continued rolling over him. Eight months after he had moved in, Norah had sat down next to him as he was playing Call of Duty on the game console she had given him for Christmas. She had placed her hand over his on the controller. "Can you stop? I've got something I want to discuss with you."

Sam killed the game, put the controller on the floor, and sank into the back of the couch. *Here it comes.*

Norah took his hands. "I'm pregnant."

Sam was stunned into silence. He shook his head as if that would change the words she'd just said. Dazed, he spit out, "Pregnant? I thought you were on the pill."

"I am. And I take them religiously. I don't know what happened. I have a doctor's appointment at the end of next week to confirm it. But I'm sure. My period is over two weeks late, and I took a test..." Her words drifted away.

"How long have you known?"

"Three days. I was trying to figure out how to tell you."

"I need some time to process this." Sam's heart was pounding. "You've had that. Let me have the same."

Sam spent two days in turmoil over Norah's news. They had never talked about children. He knew he wanted a child, but he thought it would be planned.

He took an afternoon off and totally cleaned the apartment, taking care of all his belongings that were scattered throughout the rooms and driving Norah to distraction. Her favorite dinner was in the oven and candles were glowing on the table when she walked in. He took her hand and led her to the couch. "Your news shocked me. Thank you for giving me some time." His hand moved to her belly, and he looked into her eyes. "I'm thrilled that our baby is growing in you. I love you and I want to marry you." He'd rehearsed this over and over in his mind and the words still came out much less elegantly than he'd hoped for. His eyes stayed on Norah, waiting for her to speak.

"Sam... I." Norah shook her head. "We haven't known each other long enough to talk about marriage."

"Norah, we made a baby." Sam's good mood deflated. "We knew each other well enough for that. It deserves a mother and a father."

"I was thinking about... about terminating the pregnancy. It's early. It would be a simple procedure."

Sam went from deflated to horrified and recoiled from her, pulling back his hand. "Terminate? No way. That's our *child*."

"I've been offered the job of Deputy Commissioner. It's a huge step for my career. I won't have time to care for a baby."

"I'll take care of it. My job is less demanding than yours."

"Sam." Norah huffed. "You barely take care of yourself. I mean, the apartment looks great right now, but how long did it take you just to pick up all the socks you'd left lying around? And how long will it stay like this?"

"I'll do better."

Norah rolled her eyes. "And this apartment isn't big enough for a child."

"We can buy a house."

"Sam..." she groaned.

The arguing had continued for more than a week until they went to her doctor's appointment, where the pregnancy was confirmed. The doctor asked if they wanted to hear the heartbeat and when Norah hesitated, Sam quickly answered. "Yes, we do." At the sound of the gentle whooshing, his heart jumped in a way he'd never felt before, and tears filled his eyes. Looking down at Norah, he saw the same tears, and he grasped her hand. She squeezed back tightly, and Sam knew he'd won the battle. They would be having a baby.

A Walmart sign caught his eye, and Sam checked his watch before deciding to stop. *I've got to have something for Piper to sleep on when Norah drops her off tomorrow.* As he wandered the aisles of the store, he thought about the first time he held Piper. *I won the battle but lost the war. I should have known then.*

With his shopping complete, Sam resumed the drive on secondary roads that gave way to gravel and narrowed on each turn. The memory of how Piper almost wasn't born made him nauseous, the same way it did every time he thought about it. He swallowed hard as his very dark house came into sight.

Afterword

Did you enjoy this book? If you did, leaving a review on Amazon or Goodreads is a wonderful way to let the author know. Reviews are one of the most powerful tools in an author's arsenal.

Sneak Peak

CADEN

"Hey, if you've got my number, you know my name. Leave a message and I'll call you back."

Getting her voicemail greeting rattled Caden Brady, and he ended the call without saying anything. *Damn, I hoped she'd answer. She responded to my text right away this morning. Maybe she's still on the road.*

Caden had met Quinn Michaels the day before at a conference and was instantly captivated. Conversation flowed easily between them, but make the choice to call her was next-level for Caden. He hadn't wanted to talk to a woman in a long time.

He took a deep breath and blew it out as he gazed across Boston Harbor. The weather was mild for early November, and the moon was just peeking above the horizon. Noisy seagulls scuttled along the docks, hoping for a morsel to scavenge. The waterfront teemed with restaurants, hotels and luxury condominiums. *I'll try again after dinner with the family.*

QUINN

Quinn picked up her phone and took another sip of wine as she opened her photos to look at the selfie she had taken with Sam the night before at an Italian restaurant in Boston's North End. Sam's hair was light brown, and his icy-blue eyes glowed in sharp contrast to the dark brown of Quinn's hair and eyes. Their smiles were wide, reflecting their happiness at having reconnected.

It was good to reconnect. In every way.

She closed the photo app and found five text messages from Sam.

> *Sam: Hope you got home okay.*

> *Sam: Bought those inflatable mattresses we talked about.*

> *Sam: I miss you.*

> *Sam: I was hoping to hear from you tonight.*

> *Sam: Talk tomorrow?*

Quinn shook her head, thinking of high school when they texted each other all the time.

> *Quinn: I'm home. I'm headed to bed. Catch up tomorrow.*

As she closed the messages, she noticed two missed calls. *Probably Mom, wanting to chat about my trip.* But when she looked at the list of recent calls, she was surprised to see both calls had come from private numbers. No voicemail, though.

Quinn shrugged and drained her wine glass. *If they couldn't leave a message, I guess they didn't really want to talk to me.*

The story continues in Whispers of Mistletoe, coming on November 12.

Acknowledgements

There are so many people I'm grateful to for their support in this new adventure. First, my early readers. Joanna Hastings, Rebecca Maeve Hartwell, Melinda Domings, and Evelyn Shine. You suffered through my very unpolished words and gave me gentle feedback about my obvious writing faux pas as well as suggestions which resulted in a more interesting story.

Next, the Sunday Morning Breakfast Club, Steve, Candace, Eric, Bill and Margrethe. Your interest and questions enabled me to become comfortable talking about my writing. And special thanks to Steve for answering all my technical/IT "How do I" questions.

Sally Walker and Sheryl Soffer, my critique partners---Where would I be without you? I'm so grateful to Sheryl for reaching out to an on-line stranger and to both of you for taking me in. You understood Quinn and Sam better than I did and your insights helped me shape them into the characters I wanted them to be. I hope our little group continues for many books.

I was nervous about submitting my manuscript for professional editing but so happy I took that step and that I selected Red Adept Editing. My content editor, Rashida Breen, found the plot holes which, deep in my heart, I already knew about, and gave me mechanisms to fix them. My line editor, Mary Morris, took my clumsy text and turned it into elegant prose. Thank you to both of them for being kind to me as a new author and pointing out the positives in my writing as well as the areas that needed attention. I look forward to working with Rashida and Mary in the future.

Emily Hensley of Small Fry Marketing. Our association is very new, but our conversations have done so much to invigorate my writing aspirations. Thank you.

My husband, Gordy, has listened to my long-winded descriptions of what these imaginary people are going through, for three long years and is always supportive. I'm forever grateful to him for showing me what "happily ever after" looks like.

And finally, to you, my readers, a huge thank you for reading my book. Time is our most precious commodity and that you spent some of yours on my creation means everything to me.

Also by Sue Mills

Whispers of Goodbye

To read the FREE ebook copy of Quinn and Sam's origin story,

visit my website

suemillsauthor.com

About the author

Sue is an avid reader who ventured into the writing world during the first year of the Pandemic. Her stories showcase men and women working to become whole and happy. Family plays a prominent role as do the steamy encounters which come with falling in love.

Sue is a lifelong Vermonter who counts books, sunsets, and travel as vital to her being. Mountains, from the slopes of Vermont's Green Mountains to the towering peaks of Colorado's Rockies feed her soul.

Her children are grown and flown and she's living her happily ever after with the boy she met in a college library almost fifty years ago.

Follow her on Facebook, Sue Mills – Author

Or on her website, suemillsauthor.com

Or on Instagram, suemillsauthor

And TikTok, Sue Mills, Author